Zeta 2 Reticuli

Zeta 2 Reticuli

DAVID SCOTT

Copyright © David Scott.

All rights reserved. No part of this book may be reproduced in any form or by any electronic or mechanical means, including information storage and retrieval systems, without permission in writing from the publisher, except by reviewers, who may quote brief passages in a review.

ISBN: 978-1-64669-667-3   (Paperback Edition)
ISBN: 978-1-64669-668-0   (Hardcover Edition)
ISBN: 978-1-64669-666-6   (E-book Edition)

Some characters and events in this book are fictitious. Any similarity to real persons, living or dead, is coincidental and not intended by the author.

Book Ordering Information

Phone Number: 347-901-4929 or 347-901-4920
Email: info@globalsummithouse.com
Global Summit House
www.globalsummithouse.com

Printed in the United States of America

Contents

Chapter 1: California Institute of Technology 1
Chapter 2: Massachusetts Institute of Technology 3
Chapter 3: Security Clearances 5
Chapter 4: Area 51 7
Chapter 5: Secret Date 12
Chapter 6: Sector 4 22
Chapter 7: Storm Area 51 42
Chapter 8: Harnessing Antimatter 46
Chapter 9: Bending Spacetime 51
Chapter 10: Secret Plan 53
Chapter 11: Saucer Test Flight 64
Chapter 12: Warp Factor 6 102
Chapter 13: Baby It's Cold Outside 120
Chapter 14: Calling Occupants of Interplanetary Craft 133
Chapter 15: Close Encounters of the Third Kind 144
Chapter 16: Hope has Wings 173
Chapter 17: In the Beginning 201

Chapter 1

California Institute of Technology

Twelve Years Ago.

Priscilla Waterford's parents had been taking her to a psychiatrist for two months.

"You're saying she's not autistic then, doctor?" Priscilla Waterford's anxious parents asked the psychiatrist.

The doctor double-checked the notes he'd made after a two-hour session with Priscilla.

"I'm saying she's probably within the high functioning range on the autism scale. You've told me she was precocious when she was a child and had a tendency to fixate on objects and is awkward dealing with her peers. For now, let's monitor her and please continue to keep your journal. It was very helpful. Her condition can be managed and she can lead a fairly normal life."

Priscilla's parents exchanged relieved looks.

"One thing more," the doctor added, "there is evidence of extreme intelligence. Have you ever had her IQ tested? It could be in 160s."

The Present.

Priscilla Waterford wanted to avoid her Caltech classmates who were going into a Starbucks in Pasadena and ducked into the Winchell's donut shop next door on Lake Avenue.

The last thing she needed was to engage in small talk with people she found boring and uninteresting.

Priscilla bought the same chocolate sprinkled donut and same sized coffee she always did, put in the same amount of sugar and creamer in her coffee she always did and went to her table in the corner of the donut shop.

As she was sipping her coffee a man obviously disguising his features with a hat and dark glasses entered the rear door of Winchell's from the parking lot and sat down in the empty table across from her without ordering anything.

Priscilla was feeling the man's eyes scrutinizing her.

The man got up and sat down at her table facing her gesturing for her to stay put and be quiet.

He said, "Don't accept that job with JPL."

He got up and handed Priscilla a business card that only had a phone number listed on it.

"Call that number."

He disappeared as quickly as he came.

Chapter 2

Massachusetts Institute of Technology

Twelve Years Ago.

Prescott Barr's parents had been taking him to a psychiatrist for two months.

"Is he autistic?" Prescott Barr's worried parents asked the psychiatrist.

The doctor double-checked the notes she'd made after a two-hour session with Prescott.

"He's probably a high functioning autistic. You've told me he dislikes changes in his routine and is unduly sensitive to sounds and counts objects. For now, let's monitor him and please continue to keep your diary on a daily basis. It was very informative. His condition can be managed and he can lead a fairly normal life."

Prescott's parents exchanged relieved looks.

"Oh, something else," the doctor added, "Have you had his IQ tested? My findings indicate he has an unusually high IQ. Might be in the 160 range."

The Present.

Prescott Barr was walking along Vassar Street in Cambridge, Massachusetts near the MIT campus walking between the lines on the sidewalk.

While walking Prescott decided not to attend a party being held by some of his PhD candidate classmates. He considered these events to be phony social behavior and a waste of time. Prescott found socializing with his classmates annoying and boring.

Prescott heard someone's footsteps following close behind him. Prescott glanced backwards seeing a man obviously disguising his features with hat and dark glasses walking briskly toward him.

He had an uncanny ability to detect patterns and this man's walking pace didn't fit the normal pattern.

Prescott was instantly uncomfortable feeling the man's eyes burning into the back of his head.

As he began walking faster the man suddenly caught up with him.

"No longer concern yourself with your third doctoral dissertation," the man said handing Prescott a card that only had a phone number listed on it.

"Call that number."

The man turned around and walked away.

Chapter 3

Security Clearances

Priscilla's life became like opening a can of worms after she called the number listed on the business card provided by the mysterious man. Her new name was Sandra Jenkins. Like a circus animal she now had a handler.

She was told her family would be contacted and informed.

She would be taken to a still unknown destination.

Priscilla had been given a chance to say no to her new job. She couldn't say no because the idea of working on cutting edge technology thoroughly piqued her interest.

Prescott found his life mirroring Priscilla's in lockstep. His new name was Frank Owens. Prescott had a handler just like she did.

The same censorship criteria applied to his family just as it did to hers.

Prescott found his new job opportunity undeniable. He couldn't say no and they knew it.

A man introducing himself as John Doe drove Priscilla to a plane waiting for her at LAX.

She was nervous being all alone on this unmarked jet she couldn't see out of because of blackout windows.

Arriving at McCarran International Airport at Las Vegas, John Doe helped Priscilla with her luggage and led her to a black Ford Victoria waiting on the tarmac with windows to match and no plates.

Priscilla was driven to an apartment somewhere in the Las Vegas metropolitan area.

A man introducing himself as John Smith drove Prescott to a plane waiting for him at Boston Logan International Airport.

He was nervous being all alone on this jet he couldn't see out of because of blackout windows.

Arriving at the McCarran International Airport at Las Vegas, John Smith helped Prescott with his luggage and led him to a black Ford Victoria waiting on the tarmac with windows to match and no plates.

Prescott was driven to an apartment somewhere in the Las Vegas metropolitan area.

Chapter 4

Area 51

After a couple days settling into their new separate digs, Prescott and Priscilla were picked up at their apartments by John Smith and John Doe respectfully and driven to the McCarran International Airport.

Their handlers had told Prescott and Priscilla not to speak with anyone until they were sitting in the briefing room at their new job site, wherever that was.

After being handed boarding passes with a logo at the top saying Janet Airlines, they found themselves waiting on the tarmac with about a dozen other people, all with a look on their faces saying, 'I should have taken the blue pill'.

An all-white unmarked commuter jet with blackout windows taxied up and they all boarded. As the wheels left the ground, they were relieved that this time they weren't alone for the ride to where?

Prescott and Priscilla were seated along the aisle across from each other and locked eyes for the first time.

After being airborne for fifteen minutes the plane nosed down. They felt it bank hard right, then level off for toward what seemed southeast. Could this be possible. It was aiming straight at Groom Lake Area 51.

They both snapped back at the same time and noticed each other again. Hmmm. They were going to the same place.

As the tires screeched screeched on the runway it snapped their minds back to more mundane things like is Area 51 beneath them? This strange group of blind dates exited the plane and saw two men in uniform seated behind a table set up on the tarmac.

They surrendered their IDs and cell phones to these men. They were then handed ID badges with strange markings on them.

Priscilla protested saying, "I was told I would be able to stay in touch with my family." One man replied curtly, "You will ma'am, please move along."

They were all herded onto an unmarked bus with blackout windows and driven to a building about a hundred yards away.

When they arrived, they were waved into a conference room with a podium and were told to take seats in folding chairs. Prescott and Priscilla took seats next to each other.

Four men in black circled the conference room looking like sharks in a tank. The new recruits eyed these men warily. One of the men was taking photos.

The men in black were paying attention to their hand movements.

A man in a gray suit entered from the rear and walked to the podium. All chatter ended.

The man behind the podium began speaking.

"Please look at the ID badges you received when you deplaned. You'll notice they have a colored bar on them. These bars denote the level of clearance you have. You'll be told later about the area restrictions and what the color codes mean. Observe these strictly."

He then leaned forward on the podium scanning the room.

"The military police are under orders to use deadly force with anyone found to be in an area their ID badge doesn't authorize them to be in."

The man in a gray suit man leaned back relaxing.

"You are requested and required to discuss your specific project assignments with members of your team only and nobody else. This of course being necessary for you to do your work.

I can tell you all this. You will see and do things here you never could have imagined possible. The things we do here are far beyond theories and make the Manhattan Project look like a high school chemistry experiment.

I hope you all brought your thinking caps with you. I have a feeling you'll need them.

Other than that, welcome to what we call Dreamland. But be careful," he said, "around here dreams can quickly turn to nightmares if you don't pay attention."

The screen behind him flickered to life as he repeated the words on the screen, WELCOME TO AREA 51.

Glancing at his watch, he continued.

"Spend a few minutes getting to know each other. Someone will be here soon to divide you into three person teams and tell you what your team's specific focus will be."

The room began to buzz with whispers as the man in the gray suit walked toward the rear.

On his way out he stopped and whispered to one of the men in black. The man nodded saying, "Yes sir, I understand."

Meanwhile, Prescott and Priscilla looked nervously at each other.

Prescott broke the ice saying, "Well, I guess it's ok for us to talk."

"I don't know whether to give you my new name or my real name."

"I tell you what, let's get real for a minute. I feel like I'm in The Twilight Zone."

Priscilla replied, "No kidding."

He extended his hand saying, "My real name is Prescott Barr."

Before she could take it, he jerked it back looking around the room. She pulled her hand back too saying, "Oh yeah, talk don't touch."

Prescott then said rather urgently, "I don't know how long we'll have in here right now. I know I've seen you around before and I know you've seen me. This may seem forward and I apologize, but we don't have a lot of time and I'd like to see you again under better circumstances."

Priscilla told him her real name and said, "I was thinking the same thing."

"Ok," Prescott said, "Commit this to memory."

They then verbally exchanged cell numbers and addresses quietly.

No sooner had they done this another man this time in military garb entered saying loudly, "Stand and follow me."

They glanced at each other as they rose with Prescott saying, "Good timing."

The next part of the procedure was pretty straightforward. They were all given cards with the names of the people they would be working with and told to find each other in the room.

As Priscilla and Prescott looked at their cards they smiled and found each other.

Priscila said, "This is better than any Twilight Zone I've ever seen."

After about an hour's break for lunch they all returned to the conference room.

Another man in a gray suit went to the podium. He tapped on the microphone and the room went quiet. The man started speaking without introducing himself.

"Good afternoon, ladies and gentlemen I hope you enjoyed your lunch. I'm sure you figured out you'll be working on black ops. Your ID badges reflect that. And that level is called Majestic-12. But do pay attention to the color codes because that gives you specific clearance.

With regards to the lives you had before boarding that plane, consider that you have been through what is called sheep dipping. Your records have been purged including social security numbers, IRS records, schools, driver's licenses, even your Grandma Betty's maiden name.

Your cell phones will be returned every day when leaving the base, but your carrier is now is the U.S. government. Don't worry about minutes and usage Uncle Sam will pick up the tab. I'm sure you'll understand your calls will always be monitored and tracked. You'll be provided with cars off base. Again, Uncle Sam will pay all costs gas and oil changes, etc.

The downside. Romantic entanglements are prohibited and any off-base socializing should be done very carefully. Remember, loose lips can sink spaceships too."

The rest of the day was a blur of activity for Prescott and Priscila. Directions, schedules, a complete physical including a dental examination and Lasik corrective eye surgery for which they both were grateful to jettison the thick glasses they'd worn.

Chapter 5

Secret Date

Prescott flew back to Las Vegas with Priscilla on a jet that was part of the Janet fleet. Prescott was reeling with different emotions. Is this all for real?

He entered his apartment trying to get his head around all that had happened during the last week. Then his mind turned to Priscilla.

Prescott knew romance was forbidden, but somehow this didn't bother him. He had her phone number and address and she had his. He could see the beginning of a beautiful friendship.

Prescott's mind then jumped to the task he and Priscilla had been assigned to; namely, how to bend spacetime for a craft that in three months was scheduled to take people to the moon and back in a matter of seconds, if the theories were correct.

He was grateful they weren't housed at Area 51 itself.

Prescott knew that each of them were under surveillance including phones and internet connections as was stipulated in the document they all signed waiving most of their civil rights and officially being part of a satellite government.

Now he had to find a way to contact Priscilla without being detected.

They would be working on the same team of three. His specialty was going to be gravity amplification for bending spacetime for one of the larger alien saucers that had been acquired intact.

The assignment he was going to work on was incredible.

This spacecraft was scheduled to take a warp drive test flight to the moon and back in three months.

As Priscilla entered her apartment, she too was a jumble of thoughts and emotions. Working with Prescott was more than she could have hoped for. She wondered if that was by the design of unseen hands.

As the man at the briefing had said working at Area 51 was beyond anything that she could have imagined possible.

Priscilla was going to be working on creating stable antimatter from Element 115, or from whatever the alien's used as the source for creating stable antimatter, so it could be converted into permanent stable negative energy anti-matter for the spacecraft's propulsion system that was based on gravity amplification.

Gravity amplification powered by antimatter as the spacecraft's propulsion system was the prevailing consensus.

The upcoming warp drive test flight was not without its dangers. She knew they'd been told what heroes they would be so long as they brought the ship back in one piece.

Priscilla was glad that they were able to live off base from Area 51.

Then her thoughts turned to Prescott. There was something intriguing about him. It was as if she had known him all of her life.

The security oath she and the other fourteen in the briefing had signed today including Prescott strictly forbade any fraternization with fellow employees of any kind at the risk of fine and imprisonment.

Priscilla knew that wouldn't stop them. She and Prescott would be together.

Unknown to each other Prescott and Priscilla arrived at the airport at the same time. They had been instructed to park their cars in a specially designated area.

As soon as Prescott exited his car after parking it in the secure area, he saw a car enter the parking lot, saw the person inside show an ID badge to the guard house and pull in. There was something familiar about the body language.

Prescott was pleasantly surprised as he recognized the face. It was Priscilla!

She almost lost her discipline and came close to waving to him, but caught herself just in time as she wheeled into a parking space. He continued walking forward ignoring her knowing security cameras were all over the place watching their every move.

Priscilla slowly got out of her car to give Prescott enough time to get inside the airport without drawing any attention to her or him.

Prescott found the assembly area roped off with handlers roaming about. This was going to be a tedious routine, but worth it. He sat down nonchalantly after showing one of handlers his ID badge.

There she was. They gave each other a quick stare. Priscilla checked in with a handler and found a seat that was almost across from him.

Priscilla wondered if Prescott knew Morse Code. She began to blink with both eyes as Prescott realized she was sending him signals with her blinking.

It was Morse Code! He had taught himself Morse code on a whim a few years ago to use with a friend as a secret form of communication to bypass his parents. Now she was using it to communicate with him.

He began to read the Morse code signals she was sending with her blinking eyes. Luckily, she was sitting close enough for him to read her eyes. His Lasik surgery had given him 20/20 vision which also helped greatly.

Prescott began blinking out a quick reply and an invitation as Priscilla was reading his eye blinks with her newfound 20/20 vision.

Meet Luxor eight.

Priscilla replied.

Ok.

Suddenly one of the handlers pointed in silence to Prescott, Priscilla and an older woman motioning them to follow him. They all followed their designated handler out to a waiting bus that took them to one of those Janet jets.

Prescott glanced at his reflection in the mirror, trying to look cool. He then turned away, shaking his head and muttering under his breath, "Give it up. You can't teach a pig how to sing."

It was almost time for him to head out. He wanted to be sure he got to the Luxor well before 8:00 pm because he and Priscilla hadn't had a chance to confirm anything more than meeting at the Luxor Hotel.

He wasn't going to let his paranoia spoil things. Prescott figured his wanting to check out the sights was a normal impulse.

Prescott hoped she would drive her own car, then realized that that was unlikely, considering they had tracking devices on their cars. Las Vegas Boulevard was too busy at night and it made more sense to call for a ride.

Prescott called a taxi.

He turned off his smart phone and removed the batteries, putting them in his front pocket. Hopefully that would help circumvent any secret tracking devices they might have hidden in the phone. Help, but not stop, he reasoned.

Priscilla checked herself out in the mirror wishing she had that Cosmo look, whatever that was.

As she was about to call for a taxi, she figured that the security people would have all taxi company records for base employees, and she had a feeling Prescott would assume the same.

She decided to hold off calling for the cab until 7:30 pm on the chance Prescott might be calling his ride about now. She knew Prescott like her probably wouldn't drive his own car because these cars would surely have tracking devices galore in them.

The Strip was too busy anytime, but especially at night. She knew by instinct Prescott was, like her, a practical person.

Priscilla remembered what they had all been told in the multiple briefings they'd had that first day that they would be under a microscope 24/7. Priscilla knew she and Prescott had more or less signed their lives away for the opportunity of a lifetime. The sky was literally the limit.

This oversight and scrutiny would be a real test of their endurance. Priscilla called for her ride.

She turned off her smart phone and removed the batteries, feeling this was a futile attempt at thwarting their efforts at surveillance, but any preventive action no matter how small was better than taking no action.

Prescott was waiting for his ride standing outside his apartment trying to be inconspicuous. Then he saw a car enter the complex, the driver looking around. He stepped forward and waved as the driver acknowledged and came to a stop. Prescott got in giving directions to take him to the Luxor. They sped into the Las Vegas sunset.

Priscilla was waiting for her ride standing outside her apartment wondering if she was dressed to impress. Then she saw a car driving slowly down the street, the driver scanning the sidewalk.

Priscilla waved at him. He pulled to the curb and she got in the back. Take me to the Luxor, she said. He nodded, saying yes ma'am and they were gone.

Prescott paid the driver as he got out onto the sidewalk and promenade in front of the Luxor Hotel. A good number of people were milling on the promenade. It was about a quarter past seven. He was glad he was early.

He staked out a spot underneath the obelisk in front of the hotel and was keeping his eyes peeled for his special lady. It was dusk and a beautiful evening in Las Vegas. Prescott had never felt this way before.

Priscilla was looking at the different hotels approaching the intersection of Tropicana Avenue and Las Vegas Boulevard. As they came to a stop Priscilla was watching people walking quickly in front of the New York New York hotel.

"Is the Luxor much further?" Priscilla asked the driver.

"No," the driver replied. "We're almost there. See the Excalibur over there on the corner of Reno Avenue and Las Vegas Boulevard? The Luxor is across the street from it."

Priscilla nodded her head as the light turned green. She had butterflies as the pyramid, sphinx and obelisk of the Luxor Hotel came into view.

Priscilla paid and exited the cab standing in front of this impressive pyramid-shaped hotel.

Prescott checked the time again on his watch. Glare from the cars and buildings and street lights made seeing faces challenging. He decided to walk a little staying close to the building to avoid running into fast walking pedestrians.

Prescott turned around and began walking back to the obelisk when he saw a car swerve onto the curve and stop. He strained his eyes as he watched the person get out of the car. It was Priscilla!

Just as he moved toward her a large party that had exited the Luxor Hotel swarmed his way. It looked like a wedding party. Prescott waved as Priscilla saw him and spontaneously laughing waved back.

Priscilla and Prescott met halfway as the crowd of people who had exited the Luxor collided with them before they could say anything. Two people in front of the group were holding hands. The groom had on a tuxedo and the bride had on a wedding dress. Priscilla and Prescott saw them heading for a long black stretch limousine that was waiting for them on the curb.

"It's a wedding party, Prescott," Priscilla observed. "Maybe a wedding reception," Prescott countered. Suddenly one of the people following the just married couple bumped into her. The woman had a name tag with the name Donna written on it.

The woman was radiating happiness. "Oh, pardon me, sorry," she said. Then she began talking to Priscilla and Prescott as if they were long time acquaintances of hers. "I always knew those two would get married," Donna said to them. Donna then joined the group of about thirty people who were throwing rice and shouting good wishes at the newly married couple as they were trying to get in the limo.

Priscilla reached down and picked up a placard that Donna had dropped.

"Look Prescott," she said as she read the text. "Happy Honeymoon Norma and Ralph and Best Wishes from your friends at Spendler Shoes." Prescott gestured to Priscilla to step back away from the crowd hovering around the limousine saying goodbye to the two newlyweds.

"I'm so happy to see you," Prescott said to Priscilla as she shyly moved toward him. He awkwardly reached out and took her hands and they were standing close looking into each other's eyes. "I'm happy to see you too," she said. "Where should we go?"

Prescott had an idea.

"How about let's just walk down the Strip together? I'm glad but puzzled why the handlers didn't install tracking chips underneath our skin. Maybe they put something in our shampoo."

They both laughed.

"I've been so paranoid, I turned off my phone and removed the batteries."

"I did too!" Priscilla gushed. "Sounds logical walking down the Strip with all these people walking around. You're very logical."

"Like Spock would say," Prescott said chuckling, "very logical Captain."

They began walking toward the Excalibur Hotel as their hands brushed. Prescott, unlike his typical modus operandi when it came to the opposite sex, reached out and took her hand as she squeezed his.

"Can you believe it?" Priscilla enthused. "Can you believe what we've learned?"

Prescott vigorously shook his head in disbelief. "No, I can't. It's beyond amazing. I always knew humans weren't alone in the universe."

"To think we're going to be the team who finishes up the gravity propulsion on the alien spacecraft for a test flight to the moon and back. Prescott, I'm so happy you and I were assigned to work together."

Prescott stopped walking, pulled Priscilla by her hand and moved her in position and kissed her. He had seen that done in the movies, but had never done it in real life.

They resumed walking and talking.

"Tomorrow we're going to Sector 4, or S4 as they call it, where we will be working," Priscilla said.

"I know," Prescott said. "Remember, we must only talk about our work when at work, which won't be a problem, and only use our fake names. We must be on guard to always pretend we don't know each other except as coworkers. There so much I want to know about you. Where did you go to school?"

"Caltech," she replied. "You?"

"MIT. How did you come up with the idea of blinking using Morse code?" he asked laughing. "That was so cool."

"It just came to me. I knew you'd be able to read it," she said moving close to Prescott.

"That's unbelievable Priscilla. I –," Prescott caught himself in time.

"Love you," Priscilla said, grinning as she finished his sentence for him squeezing his hand again.

They were relaxed accepting the fact of their love as if it was an immutable law of physics such as Einstein's General Theory of Relativity.

"We can use Morse code for covert communication," Prescott continued. "The handlers probably wouldn't pick up on that. I think as time goes on and as they begin to trust us, they will dial back their monitoring."

"Good idea," Priscilla said. "I wish we could go somewhere quiet to talk, but that would be too dangerous."

"We've got to play ball with the handlers for a while," he recommended. "I'm trying to think of a way we could talk and not be detected by the handlers."

"I know a way," Priscilla said as if struck by sudden inspiration. "I know a way to put our smartphones on scramble. What kind of phone to you have? Wait, an iPhone of course."

"Of course," Prescott replied. "Perfect," Priscilla said. "I know how to tweak it so we can use a temporary 888 number to chat on. I've done this before."

He had a concern. "You know the handlers always have access to our phones when we surrender them at the airport every day. You know they will routinely check them out."

"No worries. I played a prank at Caltech one time solo and none of the professors could ever figure out how their phones were compromised and who did it. Trust me no known phone spying software can defeat it. If they couldn't figure it out the handlers won't be able to figure it out. They never thought silent tiny timid little me could pull it off."

Prescott grinned at Priscilla with affection. "I had no idea you could be so mischievous. Let's do it," he said.

She motioned for Prescott to follow her over to the side of a building.

"Give me your phone and batteries," she said. Prescott did as he was instructed. "I need more light. Let's go over there," Priscilla directed. They walked over to a better illuminated area oblivious to the crowds of people acting as their camouflage.

Priscilla took out a small packet of specialty tools from her purse and set Prescott's phone on scramble. Then she set her phone on scramble.

"You carry stuff like that in your purse?" he asked watching her intensely. "You really are an egghead. Can you teach me how to do that?"

"Sure thing," Priscilla said as she showed Prescott. She reassured him that this would be undetectable.

"When you call my number, we can talk safely without detection. After we have our scrambled phone calls, we will set them back to normal. They'll be none-the-wiser."

"I'll call us a cab," Prescott said.

"I need to keep my eye on you," he said as he kissed Priscilla on her forehead.

"Right back at you," she said.

When the cab pulled up at Priscilla's apartment building Prescott ducked below the seats.

After they got home Prescott and Priscilla talked enthusiastically on the phone about the gravity amplification propulsion project they would be working on together.

A big part of their conversation centered on their mounting anticipation of their first joint visit to Sector 4 of Area 51 tomorrow that would be their permanent duty station for now.

They also decided they'd made a mistake by riding in the same cab together and took a mutual vow not to repeat it. But love can be blind.

They were both hoping there would be no negative fallout from this oversight.

They spoke for three hours until they reluctantly said goodbye. They talked about everything under the sun and some stuff beyond it.

Chapter 6

Sector 4

The next morning after arriving at Groom Lake Area 51 Prescott, Priscilla and the older woman were herded into another bus outfitted with blackout windows. They were also blindfolded asking themselves if being blindfolded before going to work would be part of their daily work routine from now on.

The handler said to the driver, "Move out!"

They were going to boldly go where no Trekkie has gone before.

A mysterious man in a gray suit was watching them from the back of the bus.

After 10 minutes of a relatively smooth ride the bus suddenly was on a rougher stretch of road jostling and bumping around its occupants for another 5 minutes as if they were in a cattle car.

The bus rolled to a shaking stop.

The handler removed their blindfolds and said, "Out of the bus."

They all hustled out of the bus looking at the base of a mountain and saw the Papoose dry lake bed in the distance.

Ten armed troops appeared out of nowhere and positioned themselves five each on both sides of the three new S4 job inductees.

Priscilla and Prescott and their third still unknown female coworker were being treated to some psychological mind games. They played along more amused than frightened.

Suddenly a section of the mountain started to disappear uncovering a large open hole in the side of the base of the mountain.

"Follow me!" the obviously ranking man in the gray suit said and they dutifully followed.

The troops stayed in formation.

They stepped onto a concrete surface area in front of the open bay door that was the entrance to a hangar.

As they entered the air-conditioned hangar, Prescott thought he detected a whiff of perfume emanating from Priscilla. The cool air was a relief from the stifling heat of the desert.

The handler stepped back as the man in the gray suit spoke one sentence in a slow, serious and measured tone.

"You know the consequences if any of you are found to be in violation of your security oaths. Follow me."

The way he spoke was more intimidating to Prescott and Priscilla and the still unnamed older woman than a raised voice.

They followed the handler and the man in the gray suit inside the mountain entrance as the large door began closing behind them.

The handler displayed his ID badge to the security guard that was scanned. The security guard also passed the scanner over his eyes and right hand.

Then he went through what looked like a passenger boarding bridge tunnel at airport security. Once through the handler turned around and signaled with his hands for Priscilla to go through.

Priscilla flashed her ID badge to the security guard who scanned the bar code and passed the scanner over her eyes and right hand. For a brief moment Priscilla could see the bones in her right hand as if looking at an x-ray.

As Priscilla was walking through the tunnel Prescott was being scanned and waved through.

Prescott walked through the tunnel as the third person on their team, the still unnamed older woman, experienced the scanning process followed by the man in a gray suit.

Once all five were through the tunnel the two men were more relaxed.

"This way," the handler said casually without raising his voice. All five sauntered toward a second wall extending to the ceiling and an entrance that was also manned by security guards who remained in their guard shacks.

A steel door whished open automatically as Priscilla and Prescott and their coworker walked in with the handler and the man in the gray suit.

They were inside a large room filled with cubicles and open work areas. Here and there people were sitting in cubicles. Half the cubicles were empty. A dozen people were working in teams of two and three in several open areas containing what appeared to be large aircraft parts. Priscilla and Prescott knew from their briefings those parts were extraterrestrial.

Here and there were people wearing uniforms, but most of the people were dressed in regular street clothing.

They were led to an office with the word GALILEO written on an affixed door placard. The first handler knocked on the door. A man wearing an Air Force uniform answered the door and asked Prescott, Priscilla and the third person inside.

The handler and the man in the gray suit who had accompanied them on the bus left.

"Please take a seat," the man in the uniform said as Priscilla, Prescott and the third person sat down in chairs facing his desk.

Two handlers were standing on each side of him as the man in the uniform introduced himself.

"I'm Colonel Niles Smith," he said. "I am your Section Chief. Please introduce yourselves."

"I'm Frank Owens," Prescott said. "My name is Sandra Jenkins," Priscilla said.

Colonel Smith nodded in acknowledgement. Looking at the third person Colonel Smith asked, "And you are?"

"I'm Susan Jones."

The Colonel began speaking.

"After this introduction we'll be taking you to the alien spacecraft you'll be working on. You all know your individual assignments regarding the areas of technical research. You all know a warp drive test flight of the propulsion system to the moon and back is planned in three months. It's an ambitious schedule and you will be burning the midnight oil.

You are all part of a team who will report to me daily and individually on your progress at various times.

When a team approach is needed to solve a problem, I will be working with you. A handler will always be with you. Your handlers will be there to accommodate you with info and equipment.

Depending on the complexity of the problem, I and others are available to lend a hand and assist.

We strive for a team approach at S4, but as I'm sure you've figured out this is all on a need to know basis.

Smiling is permitted as well as jokes, so long as they are funny."

This brought a chuckle from the three inductees.

"You've been briefed on the history of Area 51 and given a generic overview of all of the spacecraft held in storage here at S4.

What you haven't been told is the specific vehicle you'll be working on. It is twice the size of the Sport Model as it was named, which we believe was a scout ship from a mother ship that crashed in the desert near Roswell, New Mexico in 1947. The Sport Model doesn't have the same helm and navigation control panels that the larger saucer model you'll be working on has. The reinforces our belief the Sport Model was a scout ship from a larger craft.

Otherwise the saucer you'll be working on has the same basic design as the smaller Sport Model.

If this saucer is similar to the saucer that captured the Hills, and circumstantial evidence confirms this, then the home world for the Hills' craft and your saucer is in the Zeta Reticuli binary star system. We call this larger saucer the Executive Model.

During your onboarding and orientation, you yourselves have already read briefings and have been verbally briefed on these particular Ebens, a term from the acronym E.B.E. for Extra-Terrestrial Biological Entity. I will refer to these bipedal, humanoid extraterrestrial species EBE aliens from Zeta 2 Reticuli as Greys because saying Greys is easier for me to say than Ebens or EBE aliens."

Colonel Smith signaled to the two handlers standing on each side of him to exit his office.

Colonel Smith leaned forward as Prescott, Priscila and Susan were transfixed in their chairs with anticipation all leaning toward him.

"Are you ready?" Colonel Smith asked grinning broadly.

"Yes!" all three said in unison.

All three of them were ready to see a dream of a lifetime come true in person.

Colonel Smith got up from his desk and said, "Follow me!"

Prescott and Priscilla lunged from their chairs as a startled Susan got up more slowly. He knocked his ankle into the bottom rung of his chair in his élan to scramble out of the Colonel's office. Priscilla adroitly slipped in front of Prescott shoving him aside with an affectionate elbow eliciting a friendly growl from him. Susan followed behind them.

Colonel Smith was charging ahead with the three swooning newbie recruits in tow flanked by the two handlers.

They walked down a long corridor intersecting several other corridors and approached a security checkpoint. Colonel Smith followed the security procedure showing his badge to the security guard who scanned it, the Colonel's eyes and right hand. Colonel Smith then walked through a tunnel.

Once they had all passed through security another door, a large steel door, with two troops standing guard with weapons, awaited them.

Colonel Smith inserted his badge into a slot and pulled it out quickly as the door began to open.

They were awestruck as a large saucer shaped craft loomed in front of them.

The area they were in was a large hangar in the row of hangars they had passed when entering. This craft had been blasted in its side by what looked like the outline of some kind of artillery shell.

Colonel Smith began speaking as their eyes were transfixed on the saucer shaped spacecraft supported by struts equidistantly located around the bottom of the ship.

"Welcome to Hangar 7. The Executive Model you're looking at was retrieved from Aztec, New Mexico in 1948.

It is believed that either radar or some geological anomaly temporarily knocked out their gravity amplifiers, but that is not important right now. They were at the wrong place at the wrong time. That is ironic considering how far they'd traveled in space only to crash and be killed on Earth far from home.

The Executive Model was damaged on one side by the impact of the crash. We were able to do some body work and push it back into place like it was. The interesting thing is that as we did this, the metal reformed to its original configuration naturally. The only residual evidence of the damage is the slight distortion you see on the side there," Colonel Smith said pointing.

"There was no observable damage internally. The craft has no seams, no rivets and no weld joints. We haven't identified the metallic baseline. It looks and feels like lightweight, indestructible aluminum or stainless steel. There is a group of metallurgists working on this. The external damage was repaired rather quickly.

Five of the six gravity amplifiers were undamaged. Fortunately, the damage wasn't greater. We think we've repaired the one amplifier that was damaged. Like the outside metal, it basically reconfigured itself as we did our work.

We still haven't mastered some of its complexities for the warp jumps we plan in the coming test flight in November to the moon. Gravity wave amplification is your area of expertise Frank (*Prescott*). You must find a way to giving us a high probability this will all work. If you don't, the test flight will have to be aborted.

We believe the reactor on this craft as all the crafts works on matter-antimatter. We must synthesize Element 115 in order to have a propulsion source for flying the ship, or find the alien's equivalent. It is the source for power and the gravity wave needed to amplify for bending spacetime. That is your area of expertise Sandra (*Priscilla*).

Particle accelerators, or super colliders, in Europe and the US are working overtime on this.

We have our own particle accelerators here at Area 51 that are highly classified and should be of great help.

Some of the alien spacecraft had been successfully flown within Earth's atmosphere, but became unstable as they moved away from Earth's mass. As a result, test flights have been limited to the restricted airspace around Groom and Papoose lakes and the surrounding mountains.

Frank (*Prescott*) another one of your jobs is to find out why the craft is unstable as it leaves the Earth's atmosphere.

We have learned from our short test flights how to control and navigate the ship. It seems to work in phase with the Earth's gravity, but as it moves away must somehow become independent and focus on another gravity source.

Susan, your area of expertise will be applied to finding out the gravity amplifiers tie into the helm and navigation. You must find a way to understand how this works. If you don't the test flight will have to be aborted and rescheduled for when we do understand.

This energy pulse appears to be electricity, although it seems to work backwards from all our electrical principals. The reactor appears to be passively active and it's a mystery how it has lasted all these years. Even though no one was home, the lights were still on.

This power creates all the windows and the control panels that appear shortly after anyone goes on board the ship. In other words, solid walls become windows.

We believe the writing that is displayed is for basic control identification and a few detailed instructions. Susan, I will provide you with the full translations. The translations are not guaranteed to be totally accurate until we find a Rosetta Stone, so use it as a reference tool.

Frank (*Prescott*) and Sandra (*Priscilla*), if something comes up and you think any translations could potentially help you in your work let me know and I will clear the way. Translations are provided on a need to know basis. Susan is cleared to see all of the writing because they seem to be associated primarily with the tie in of the gravity propulsion system to the helm and navigation stations.

Top linguists say this writing is like a combination of ancient Egyptian hieroglyphics, Japanese characters and the Hebrew alphabet.

The Sport Model saucer is available as a reference resource. I will need one days' advance notice if you need to see it. If it's an urgent request, then we can probably make an exception.

We've decided not to test fly Sport Model anymore. It is too valuable as an engineering reference model because it is the only alien vehicle in our possession that is completely functional at this time. We no longer wish to risk having it badly damaged beyond repair during a test flight. We've already lost several saucers because of tests and accidents of one kind or the other.

The average height of the Greys is four feet with slender bodies. We will be refitting parts of the interior to accommodate two humans a little below average height and weight meaning you, including sleeping quarters and restroom.

The test flight to the moon and back won't last long enough for sleep or hopefully use of the restroom. Nevertheless, the bunks and toilets will be retrofitted accordingly because if the test flight to the moon is successful, then the sky's the limit. I should say, then the galaxy's the limit."

Colonel Smith let out a slight chuckle.

"When that happens sleeping quarters and restrooms will be necessities."

Colonel Smith had an afterthought.

"The toilet and urinal auto-flush. They still work after all these years. We don't know exactly where the water comes from. It could be recycled. The water always tests fresh and not brackish. Yes, they use water good old H2O for toilets and apparently for drinking."

Colonel Smith let out another slight laugh as did his audience when he said, "Don't ask me about their T.P." He added, "We think it's more like a bidet."

Everyone started laughing. He then said, "Only with some kind of zapper, not water."

Everyone stopped laughing.

Colonel Smith let out another slight chuckle.

"Yes, they had to sleep and had to go to the bathroom just like us. As you already know the Greys are a gendered species of humanoids because four of the eight deceased Greys found at the crash were female, but their restroom seems to be gender neutral meaning unisex, although a urinal along with a toilet are present. You can draw your own conclusions.

To my knowledge all of the other alien craft we've recovered contained only male crewmembers. Why this craft had male and female crew members in equal numbers of four is an interesting question.

They eat and drink like us. We discovered from the translation documents where they cooked their food. Maybe they had some kind of Star Trek food replicator. We also know where they did their laundry and where they disposed of their trash. What we don't know is how the controls are enabled. Another more basic problem is there's no power running to these units."

Colonel Smith paused and smiled.

"We didn't find any coffee makers on board. Maybe there's a Starbucks between there and here. I wouldn't be surprised."

Priscilla, Prescott and Susan laughed.

He continued.

"We found a sick bay. It appears they were prepared for surgery. They may have all been skilled in doctoring.

One of the most fascinating aspects of the ship is they use what I will call free energy. Years ago, a technician brought a battery powered transistor radio onto the saucer while doing some work and it burned out. We've discovered that items that take battery power or electric power don't need them while inside the ship. How this is done remains a mystery. It could be some aspect of Nikola Tesla's energy from the vacuum theory.

Why the food replicator and what looks to be their washer and dryer can't use this free energy is another mystery, unless they are tied directly into ship's operations and bypass whatever it is exactly that generates the free energy in the first place.

They have an ambient temperature of 77 degrees Fahrenheit. You'll find it's comfortable if slightly on the warmer side. Their air is almost the same as ours. It is purified in some unknown way. The air circulates ship wide. We don't yet know how, but it works.

The lighting dims for 15 hours and then brightens for the next 15 hours back and forth. This lighting cycle always holds. Their planet which for lack of a better term I'll call Serpo is about the same distance from their star as the Earth is from the sun. Their star is about the same size as the sun.

The bottom level contains six gravity wave amplifiers and what we believe is a matter anti-matter reactor centered between them. We think they maintain artificial gravity in flight by use of the gravity amplifiers on the bottom level. Hopefully you will be able to confirm this.

During the last week before the test flight you will be doing simulation training on their helm guidance and navigation systems and take a flight simulator test. Susan, you will be focusing on this. You have a very important task ahead of you. We may need to adjust some of the parameters in the simulators based on any new findings you may uncover.

Each of you is a qualified private pilot. You three are in a unique position among the four other teams we've assembled and who are assigned to other projects at S4. For the test flight of the Executive Model we will be choosing two pilots at the end of the flight simulator training. Those two pilots will be chosen among you three.

Unfortunately, one of you will have to stay behind. The pilot selection decision will be made on the day of the flight simulator training exam based on your test scores.

As you all already know they are able to manipulate spacetime by pulling it forward allowing them to go faster than the speed of light without violating Einstein's laws of relativity. The aliens must obey these laws just as we do."

Colonel Smith waved his hands for the group to come in closer. The two handlers were standing to the side carefully watching Prescott, Priscilla and Susan.

Colonel Smith began walking around the circumference of the Executive Model talking excitedly about the ship's dimensions, etc.

"The bottom level contains six gravity wave amplifiers and what we believe is a matter anti-matter reactor centered between them.

There seems to be two different propulsion systems. One they use in phase with a planet's gravity, and one they use once they leave its gravitational influence. Frank (*Prescott*), that falls under your umbrella.

The middle level has the bridge. There are six seats. Two seats are forward behind a long console and we believe they are helm and navigation. This is where the speed of what I will call warp factors are engaged along with flight path direction.

The top level has a hatch and a crawl space leading to what I call a warp coil or warp guide nacelle to probably create a warp bubble using Star Trek terminology. These warp coils have been tentatively determined to be linked to navigation and helm control.

The top level may have a focusing element for the gravity amplifiers below. Frank (*Prescott*) has prime responsibility for this aspect of the project.

The Greys had a command structure. The deceased Greys at Roswell and Aztec had hash mark insignias on their uniform sleeves probably denoting rank and job specialty. As you may remember from one of the briefing books you read, we think we've been able to identify this. It is remarkably similar to the rank structure used by the U.S. Navy.

Three seats are arranged in the middle with only a small console present mounted in front of the seat on the right. The captain probably sat in the middle. The first officer sat next to him on the right. A third seat is available for an observer, an assistant or whomever. It could be for engineering.

There doesn't seem to be a specific section of the craft devoted to engineering like a main engineering section. Possibly all Greys are trained to be technicians or engineers. We don't know.

The stable antimatter propulsion for the gravity wave amplification might be partly, or fully, automated. The ship itself may do a lot of its own thinking.

Behind the captain was what we think is a control panel for weapons control. One seat is behind this panel. We're thinking the gravity amplifiers, or some of them, may also have been used as weapons. We just don't know.

Based on our interactions with the Greys they had and hopefully still have no hostile intentions toward humanity. The briefing books you saw explained all that and there's no need for me to repeat it.

The middle level includes the restroom, sleeping quarters, first aid station or sick bay and the galley.

The sleeping quarters, or bedrooms, have bunks, chairs and desks mounted to the floor. We have a metallurgical team at work to remove them so we can replace them with more ergonomically sized equivalents for humans. This also applies to the chairs at the helm and navigation stations. We may not tamper with the captain's chair because it appears to be directly linked to vital control systems. Same goes for the first officer's chair."

Colonel Smith engaged in a final quick pep talk before taking Prescott, Priscilla and Susan inside the Executive Model.

"Each one of you are the best in your field. If you weren't, you wouldn't be standing here with me now. People with a lot of institutional knowledge have died or retired. We videotaped their knowledge and those videos are available to you as another reference resource.

Majestic-12 is of the opinion time is of the essence if we are to get the necessary breakthroughs that are needed to back-engineer the technology and get to the moon and back. If all goes well, then it won't take but a blink of the eye for this to be accomplished.

We are counting on your dedication, hard work, loyalty, engineering and scientific knowledge to keep us on track for the test flight.

I don't know about you but when this is successful, I am going to take a long vacation and expect to be in a much higher tax bracket."

Colonel Smith theatrically removed a small remote-control device looking like a key fob, pointed it toward the saucer and pressed a button.

A door on the side of the saucer silently opened and a ramp silently pushed out extending forward then folded downward touching the ground.

Colonel Smith stood at the bottom of the ramp to the open door leading to the interior of the Executive Model.

He paused for dramatic effect, staring at the three of them.

Colonel Smith said quietly, "Shall we go inside?"

"Yes!" Prescott, Priscilla and Susan said enthusiastically.

"Follow me in then!" Colonel Smith said with military panache.

Prescott said to Priscilla and Susan, "Ladies first."

Awestruck and thrilled, Priscilla, Susan and Prescott followed Colonel Smith inside.

The two handlers followed behind.

They stepped into a circular corridor that appeared to arch around the entire spacecraft. There were open entrances without doors spaced at regular intervals. Everything was metallic silver blue in appearance the walls, the floor and the ceiling.

Colonel Smith began to speak after checking his watch.

"The distance from the floor to the ceiling in the corridor is 6 feet 5 inches. We'll go to the bridge first. We don't know the metal alloy this ship is made of. What we do know it is lightweight and incredibly strong and durable."

Colonel Smith turned to the right and led them down a few yards, then he turned to the left walking through one of the open entrances.

"This is the bridge. As you can see it is high enough in here for the average person to stand in."

They walked down into a slightly recessed area. There was a panel with two small chairs or seats behind it.

"This is the helm and navigation. Notice how small the chairs are. They are designed for someone whose height is no more than four feet. Because Sandra (*Priscilla*) and Susan are slightly taller by a foot you might be able to sit in it. Sandra (*Priscilla*), try to sit in the chair."

Priscilla scurried forward and slid her thin body in between the darkened control panel console in front of her and the chair on the right that was affixed to the floor. With great effort Priscilla was able to squeeze her body into the chair her knees crammed into and touching the underside of the panel.

Prescott said directly to Priscilla, "How does it feel?"

He instantly recognized his mistake and quickly said to Colonel Smith, "I apologize sir."

Colonel Smith looked at Prescott and said nothing.

Priscilla was looking at the control panel marveling that an alien had sat at this very station.

"Sandra (*Priscilla*), you're sitting at what we think is navigation," Colonel Smith said. Turning to Susan, he said, "We will need your expertise to confirm this."

Priscilla looked at the darkened console that had the outline of monitor screens. Suddenly several different screens lit up.

"That is the residual energy initiating after motion sensors of some kind detected our presence that I've told you about. The screens aren't active, but they are somehow receiving an energy pulse possibly electricity."

Priscilla stared at the glowing blank screens that had a green luminescent appearance. Priscilla couldn't contain herself and said, "This is so amazing!"

Priscilla resumed her placid exterior and reluctantly squeezed out of the cramped seat with some effort from under the console skinning the top of her knees. She extracted herself and stood back up.

He walked over to three chairs situated a few feet behind the two chairs at the helm and navigation console.

"If you recall from my overview the captain's chair is in the center. To the captain's right is the first officer's chair, or the second in command's chair. You see it has a control panel in front. The chair on the captain's left is possibly for observer's like the medical officer or chief engineer."

Colonel Smith whirled around. "Look," he said, pointing.

A large screen situated about twelve feet in front of the helm and navigation stations was glowing in the same green luminescence as the screens where Priscilla had been sitting.

"Keep watching," Colonel Smith said to Priscilla, Prescott and Susan, looking at his watch.

The front of the ship changed into what seemed like a picture window. They saw the hangar through the transparency.

They all let out sighs of wonder.

"Every seven minutes after someone enters this spacecraft that large screen turns into a window to the outside. It's exactly seven minutes no more no less."

Colonel Smith let the three take this in.

"We think the material the craft is made of has different properties that allow it to become transparent. The metallurgical team is looking into it. We've been trying to figure it out for decades."

Colonel Smith walked to the lone chair and work station behind the captain's chair that was slightly elevated. "As I told you earlier this could be a weapons station."

"Look!" Prescott screamed out forgetting himself. Two window openings had appeared on each side of the circular shaped bridge. They both looked out onto the outside corridor that circled the ship.

Colonel Smith walked over to one of the windows.

"See the glowing green writing on the panel adjacent to this window? Our translators believe they are emergency instructions about this and that. As I've already mentioned translations are available to Frank (*Prescott*) and Sandra (*Priscilla*) on a need to know basis. Susan, you will be given the full translations for your work."

Prescott and Priscilla stared in awe at the writing that looked like ancient Egyptian hieroglyphics.

"Let's go to the living quarters," Colonel Smith said, leading the group away from the bridge turning left back into the corridor.

They walked down the corridor following Colonel Smith who turned left again into another area about the same size as the bridge.

"Those are the two bedrooms," he said as Prescott, Priscilla and Susan peered inside.

"Notice the bunks have two beds, but as you can see, they are designed for beings who are four feet tall on average. Check out the small desk and chair."

Each bedroom contained two bunks with two beds each and a desk and chair. The bunks, desks and chairs were fixed into the floor.

"Like I told you when we were outside, we don't know if the males slept in one bedroom and the females slept in another bedroom. Maybe married couples shared a bedroom if they have marriage."

Colonel Smith guided them around the corner into an area that had an entrance that had apparently been designed with a modicum of privacy in mind.

"This is the restroom. As you can see, they don't have a stall for the toilet. As I've already said the toilet automatically flushes based on motion sensors."

On another wall was a urinal like you would see in any average men's room on Earth. The toilet and urinal were designed for four-foot aliens. On a third wall were two small sinks although water faucets weren't visible.

"Water is jettisoned from the sink by hand motion. The water is cold. If they had hot water, none is coming out."

Colonel Smith led the group away from the restroom back out into the open area.

Situated between the two bedrooms and the restroom was a table about five feet in length that stuck out from the wall.

"We believe this is the sick bay. If the doctor had to perform surgery or do a medical examination, this is where it would be done most likely on this table. The translations support this conclusion. See the glowing writing above the monitor screen?"

Colonel Smith gestured to luminescent writing next to a monitor screen above the table.

He pulled the table forward and it separated from the wall.

"We think if the doctor needed to turn the table he just pushed or pulled it in the direction needed and it complied. The table automatically returns to the wall when released."

Colonel Smith demonstrated by letting the end of the examination table go as it retracted and gently swooshed back into its original position in the wall.

Another table about ten feet in length was surrounded by eight chairs affixed to the floor with four chairs on one side and four chairs on the other side.

"This is where they ate their meals," Colonel Smith said. "We have eating and drinking utensils that were found on the floor near the table after the ship crashed. I'll make a note to show them to you sometime. They are in storage. They used an eating utensil that was a combination fork, knife and spoon all in one. They had cups that look exactly like ours with handles."

Prescott, Priscilla and Susan were flabbergasted by all they had seen and heard. To say it was surreal was a vast understatement.

Colonel Smith smiled as he looked at their faces. He'd seen that look before with other recruits to Area 51 when they saw the inside of an alien craft for the first time. Colonel Smith could tell through years of experience all three of these new recruits would be highly motivated in their jobs.

Colonel Smith walked back between the two bedrooms and the restroom and ten feet or so away from the sick bay surgical table. He took out the same small remote-control looking device he'd used to open the door to the saucer and pointed it toward the ceiling. A small hatch suddenly opened.

"This device I'm holding was found at the crash site in 1948. It's never failed to work. We have no idea how it is powered, or how it has maintained its power for all of these years, or how it triggers the entrance door to the craft and this hatch. We know it emits a radio frequency, but we don't know how that frequency is received by the ship and activates and opens the door."

Colonel Smith decided to allow his new team of three a few minutes to absorb what they'd seen.

The three of them all had the same expression. A deer in headlights.

Colonel Smith laughed to himself at seeing this look.

He resumed talking.

"As I mentioned earlier the hatch is in what we call the top level. The hatch leads to a crawl space to what we believe are focusing elements for the gravity generation below, and perhaps a weapon.

Once in there doesn't seem to be a way to turn around you'd have to crawl until you reach the hatch from the other direction. There might be another hatch we don't know about. This hatch was discovered by accident because it was open when the saucer crashed. It's about two feet high and three feet wide."

Colonel Smith smiled at them again as the three of them stood frozen in place and speechless.

"Let's go down to the bottom level now," he said.

Colonel Smith walked over to a solitary open door toward the back of the bridge behind what was thought to be the weapons station.

"Be careful. The step ladder down to the bottom level is designed for four-foot humanoids."

Colonel Smith carefully negotiated the ladder reaching the floor. "Next!" he cried out.

Prescott descended, followed by Priscilla and then Susan. Prescott helped them with their footing.

The bottom level was as large as the total area of the bridge and living quarters area on the middle level.

There was a large cylinder in the center of the floor surrounded by three smaller cylinders on each side.

Colonel Smith began explaining.

"What you see in the very center is the matter antimatter reactor. This is the power source for the saucer as well as the source for the gravity amplification to propel the saucer. Element 115 is the key. It is somehow used for both these functions. There is a huge effort around the world, secretly of course, to synthesize and collect Element 115 as we speak.

Sandra (*Priscilla*) we are counting on you to figure out how to get a stable matter antimatter reaction. Stable antimatter is required as the propulsion source for the gravity amplification to propel the saucer. If we can't do it, the test flight will have to be cancelled and rescheduled when we can do it.

We believe they used what we call Element 115, but our 115 must be synthesized and has a short half-life. We think there is a trace residue of antimatter in the reactor we've been hesitant to use because once it's gone it's gone.

Element 115 is not naturally occurring here on earth, but it may be where they come from. We just don't know. We do know almost beyond any doubt antimatter is what these craft use as a power source to amplify gravity waves.

We believe the Sport Model has some of their original antimatter left in it, but only in a small amount. We've not been able to isolate their original antimatter conclusively. As we've discussed we've flown the Sport Model and other saucers on short flights at Area 51.

We don't know how long any fuel within the reactor would last. If we tried a warp jump without knowing how long the antimatter in the reactor would last, a crew could find itself stranded from Earth and may never able to return to Earth if they couldn't repeat the warp drive jump.

So, for whoever goes it will be like going on a long trip driving with a broken fuel gauge. No one said that exploration and discovery was a safe career. Want safe? Sell printer paper over the phone."

They all filed pass the reactor wondering if it might be more like a headstone.

Colonel Smith began explaining again.

"We believe the six cylinders you're looking at are six gravity amplifiers. We believe energy created within the reactor from stable antimatter is channeled to these amplifiers causing a distortion in spacetime allowing the saucer to travel faster than the speed of light.

How different warp jumps are calibrated is something we hope you as our new eyes and ears can figure out.

Frank (*Prescott*), we are counting on you to find out the details of exactly how the gravity amplifiers work."

The three walked around these units as if they were looking at the Statue of Liberty holding the Eiffel Tower in one hand while sitting atop the Sphinx.

Colonel Smith added another pep talk to his final remarks.

"Only the top three candidates among fifteen were chosen for the Executive Model team. This is something for which all three of you can be enormously proud.

If you can pull this off, you'd better have something ready that will top, 'One small step for a man, one giant leap for mankind'."

Chapter 7

Storm Area 51

Priscilla and Prescott were talking on their secure phone line as they did every day at varied prescheduled times for the last month. Despite Priscilla's conviction that her custom phone call scrambling and location suppression software shielded them from detection, they wanted to avoid calling patterns.

Sometimes they spoke after midnight. Sometimes around eight in the evening. Sometimes just before they left home for work, or after they'd gotten home from work.

They were discussing the Facebook post called 'Storm Area 51, They Can't Stop All of Us' which hadn't turned out to be the blitzkrieg that had been anticipated.

Colonel Smith had mentioned it in passing a few times and said the U.S. Air Force would take whatever steps were necessary to neutralize any intrusions into Area 51.

"You don't think they'd actually shoot anyone who violated the perimeter, do you?" she asked.

"I don't know," he replied, "You and I know full well what's at stake. There are alien spaceships at Area 51 and alien bodies are in storage at Los Alamos and Wright-Patterson. The Air Force isn't taking this lightly. Just imagine if any of this information got out. Church attendance would go up. Wall Street would be a carnival ride, etc. No. I think the M.P.'s orders would be pretty clear. Shoot the camera first, then the cameraman and anyone else who is over the line."

"I agree," Priscilla replied. "I saw on the news where hundreds of people have been gathering along the Extraterrestrial Highway in and around Rachel, Nevada using the Little A'Le'Inn and the Alien Travel Center as bases. Some have campers and are making a tail gating party of it."

Prescott replied, "We'll see I guess."

D-day for 'Storm Area 51' began normally enough. Prescott and Priscilla arrived at McCarran International Airport as always, boarded their buses and were driven to their assigned Janet aircraft for the daily shuttle flight to Area 51.

Several hundred people had taken 'Storm Area 51' seriously and were gathered along Nevada State Route 375 also known as the Extraterrestrial Highway. A few campers and recreational vehicles were strewn across the adjacent desert.

A helicopter was flying above the crowd. A dozen troops and sheriff's deputies were poised along the base perimeter.

The jet touched down.

"Vacate the plane," one handler said as always. They shuffled out of the plane and walked directly to their waiting bus and climbed in without fanfare. It was all routine procedure now.

The bus hit the road for the daily trip from Area 51 proper down to S4.

The bus ride began normally enough.

Suddenly the radios the two handlers always carried with them came to life with a jumble of orders Prescott and Priscilla couldn't understand with the handlers replying, "Acknowledged Papa Bear."

Priscilla gasped and violated the still enforceable rule about no talking while in transit to S4 by saying, "Look!"

Two motorcycles came out of nowhere and were following the bus. The handlers removed their side arms. The motorcycles were flying American flags and sign flags reading 'We Deserve At Least One Alien' and 'Show Us Them Aliens'.

The sound of a helicopter suddenly filled the bus as a loud voice from the chopper began to talk.

"You are trespassing on United States Government property. Turn back now or deadly force will be used."

The bus began speeding up. A loud explosion startled Prescott and Priscilla and Susan as the bus blew a tire and careened off the road coming to a bumpy halt as the two motorcycles sped past them.

"Everyone ok?" one of the handlers screamed out.

"Yes," came the replies.

"Stay here!" the handlers yelled as they bounded out of the bus to interdict the trespassers. One of the handlers stopped and screamed, "Put your masks on now!" as he quickly put his on.

Prescott, Priscilla and Susan put on their gas masks as ordered and were content to watch the unfolding action from inside the bus.

The two motorcycles were turning around on the dirt road. The motorcycles were charging toward them as the helicopter that had been hovering over them suddenly sprayed an orange looking mist down on them.

The motorcycles spun out throwing the riders off.

Prescott, Priscilla and Susan watched as the helicopter landed disgorging troops who scooped up the injured men, threw them into the chopper and shouted, "Clear."

In a gust of dirt, the helicopter was in the air again.

In the meantime, the two handlers had been changing the blown tire. They finished up and ran into the bus telling the driver, "Move out!"

The bus surged ahead to S4.

Colonel Smith told them later that day the two motorcyclists who'd chased them were the only security breach into Area 51. After receiving medical treatment, the two riders had been arrested for trespassing.

For the most part Storm Area 51 had been a peaceful and festive event.

Chapter 8

Harnessing Antimatter

Ten days later Priscilla was finishing up a phone discussion with Prescott. Her speech was pressured and she was stumbling over her words like she was sharing all of the chemistry knowledge in the universe during one phone call.

"Whatever you just said. imagine I'm a dope. Could you give that to me in plain English?" Prescott requested.

"Sorry about that. You know how it is when you get all excited about something."

"Just give me the five-cent version of how you synthesized the 115."

Priscilla took a deep breath.

"Ok. This morning working on the reactor in the Executive Model I discovered this. The reactor uses magnetic containment fields of a kind I've never seen before to keep the matter and antimatter apart. If I can duplicate it tomorrow, we won't blow ourselves to smithereens when we push the button.

I asked Colonel Smith if I could take a portable particle accelerator with me to the reactor in the Sport Model in Hanger 6 next door. The particle accelerators they have are unbelievable by the way. Talk about a smart phone.

That way I was able to get some of the 115 from the Sport Model's reactor and test it in the Executive Model. I was able to isolate and stabilize the Grey's counterpart to our Element 115 Moscovium. It's the same stuff. It's probably something native to their planet, but it's the same 115. It was stable antimatter. Don't ask me how I did it because I'm not sure myself. Well, I'm sure, but as you said, you're a dope."

"How did you pitch this to him?" Prescott wanted to know.

"I made up some B.S. and he bought it. Remember Pres, he knows he has to trust us to some extent. He has no idea what we're dealing with. I'm not going to document it because I don't dare. We don't want it documented."

"You got that right we don't want it documented. That's fantastic! I won't ask the details. I did say give me the five-cent version.

Do we have enough 115 in the reactor to sustain a flight to Zeta 2 Reticuli?" Prescott inquired, thinking about the broken gas gauge comment by the Colonel.

"More than enough," Priscilla responded confidently. "I think the saucer could travel 2,000 light years on the 115 that's sitting in the reactor that nobody but you and me knows is there. It's gassed up and ready to go."

"Did you tell anyone?" Prescott asked worriedly.

"C'mon. What do you think I am? A dope?"

"No, that's me" Prescott said, relieved. "Did anyone understand what you were doing?"

"No. A handler was with me who's a chemist, but I was sly. I fudged the daily status log."

"Very good," Prescott said in admiration. "That's amazing. Can you cook?"

Prescott and Priscilla came to a simultaneous conclusion and blurted out at the same time.

"Are you thinking-?"

They laughed. They asked each other the same question again at the same time.

"Are you thinking-?"

They laughed again.

"You go first," Prescott said, since Priscilla had the doctorate in chemistry.

"Why don't we fly the saucer to the fourth planet around Zeta 2 Reticuli the alien Grey's home world?" she asked him matter-of-factly trying to be glib to tease him.

Prescott let out a long whoop completely out of character with his normally reserved personality. Priscilla doubled over laughing at Prescott and began coughing.

While they were both laughing themselves into a frenzy, Prescott said between bellows, "We'll mail 'em a postcard saying, 'Having a ball. Wishing you were here'."

They both laughed harder.

Prescott and Priscilla were seen by their friends and family as conservative, introspective nerds. If they could see them now.

"Now I know why you went to the Sport Model first to get as much 115 as you could to add to whatever 115 is left in the Executive Model. Keep at it tomorrow," Prescott said, "and keep me informed you sly girl you."

Priscilla's assigned handler, a chemist himself, was casually slouched in a chair in the bottom level of the saucer, munching from a bag of Cheetos.

She was fortunate he wasn't paying much attention, because he was supposed to be transcribing every word of their conversations and making notes on everything she did.

Oh well, she thought, let him have his snack while I figure out how to steal this thing.

Priscilla let out an involuntary snicker as the handler kept stuffing Cheetos in his face.

Lady luck was giving Priscilla an assist.

"Are you going to begin the proton bombardment soon?" the handler asked her.

Priscilla glanced over the particle accelerator at the handler nervously because she was about to lie and deceive on an epic scale. "Yes, soon," she answered.

Priscilla thought quickly.

"I'm ready now," she said.

The handler got up, wiping the yellow off his fingers and walked over.

She repeated the results of the test she'd made yesterday and now knew for sure stable antimatter could be created for use as an energy source in the saucer's reactor. Priscilla felt a surge of intense excitement.

Priscilla, through feeding the handler physics tensor calculus double-talk that sounded believable was good enough to freeze his brain for four minutes. The time it took to conduct the test and give her a lead-in to what she was really trying to do without him getting suspicious.

Her handler looked at the readouts on the particle accelerator and at her bogus status log and he had a question.

"Did we create a stable antimatter half-life for four minutes before decay?"

"Yes. I think we can create just enough antimatter for the warp test flight to the moon and back. Four minutes should be enough time for the flight."

The handler was watching Priscilla, who was spouting out made-up technical readings as she wrote them down for the benefit of the handler.

Priscilla continued with more physics double-talk as the handler pretended to understand what she was saying, which was gobbledygook sprinkled with a few facts for realism.

"Colonel Smith will want to speak with you. Come with me."

She followed the handler feeling pleased with herself.

Priscilla was beginning to enjoy this subterfuge.

She was considering challenging Prescott to a friendly poker game in the future. For money.

Priscilla had an hour-long meeting with Colonel Smith giving an academy award winning performance.

"I was able to transmute Element 115 into stable antimatter for four minutes," Priscilla told Colonel Smith as he was going through her log entries. "It's not stable in the strict sense of the word, but stable enough to do the warp drive field test to the moon and back."

"This is a breakthrough," Colonel Smith told her. "It's too bad you won't get a Nobel prize for it. This information is still too sensitive. We'll see what the Brass thinks after this flight."

Pretending a need to look at the helm and navigation consoles where Prescott and Susan were working Priscilla managed to blink a Morse code message to him:

Stable.

"You really fooled them?" Prescott asked Priscilla in disbelief during their scrambled phone call that night.

"I did," Priscilla replied. "Even Colonel Smith was convinced and he's an MIT graduate like you."

"Was that a Caltech jab? Seriously, you done good girl. Not only discovering how to create stable antimatter for the reactor, but being able to fool that chemist and Colonel Smith, a top-notch MIT physicist, into believing you'd discovered how to create Element 115 antimatter for four minutes."

Now it was his turn to step up to the plate and make sure he found a way to make gravity amplification work for interstellar spaceflight.

They were going to steal a flying saucer.

Chapter 9

Bending Spacetime

In the bottom level of the saucer in front of their two handlers, one who was taking notes, Prescott and Susan were discussing how it all worked.

"So," as Prescott continued, "We know there is energy in the vacuum of space itself. It's the energy generated by the vibration of spacetime. It is also tied to gravitational fields because special relativity tells us energy and mass are equivalent."

Susan was walking around the reactor talking to Prescott.

"In order to warp spacetime an electromagnetic field of sufficient power and energy density needs to be joined with the local spacetime field. The energy density of the electromagnetic field has to be such that it directly impinges upon the vacuum energy of the spacetime field. Vacuum energy is nothing more than the popping in and out of existence of particle/virtual particle pairs generated by the fluctuations of the field as predicted by quantum theory."

"Exactly," Prescott responded. "A bubble of spacetime containing the saucer is being moved along when spacetime is contracted ahead of the ship and expanded behind the ship. A nested field structure is created with the warping gradient decreasing from front to back and from outer to inner field creating the pushing effect."

Prescott paused, and shared a final thought.

"The gravity wave gets formed at the sphere by antimatter and extends the strong nuclear force or gravity wave beyond the atoms they're in. The wave guide siphons off the gravity wave that's channeled above the top level of the saucer to the bottom level here where there are six gravity amplifiers, which amplify and direct the gravity waves creating its own gravitational field."

Susan looked at Prescott.

"I've figured out how the helm and navigation work and how they tie into the reactor. Let's go back upstairs and I'll show you the basic controls."

Chapter 10

Secret Plan

Susan was a threat looming on the horizon. Because Susan's expertise was in gravity propulsion and its relationship to helm and navigation there was a high degree of probability she would be chosen as one of the two pilots for the November test flight.

Prescott estimated there was a seventy-one percent chance Susan would be one of the two pilots among the three of them selected for the test flight.

When it came down to the choice between him and Priscilla as the second pilot, Prescott estimated he had an eight percent edge in probability of being selected over Priscilla.

Prescott knew one fact. He wasn't going to Zeta 2 Reticuli with Susan and neither was Priscilla.

"What are we going to do about Susan?" Prescott asked Priscilla on their secured phone line.

"I don't know, but we'd better do something, and soon."

"I've got an idea," he said. "If you can find stable antimatter, I can pull this off with my psychology training. I'm going to hypnotize her."

The both laughed.

He added, "It won't hurt her a bit. I may even add a post-hypnotic suggestion and tell her that she isn't so uptight."

The next day Prescott and Susan were working in the bottom level again with handlers close by as always.

Prescott was going to be drifting far outside his comfort zone in order to begin executing Phase 1 of the plan to neutralize Susan. He remembered what he'd studied about method acting and then psyched himself up.

As they were about to climb the ladder back up to the middle level Prescott asked Susan in front of the handlers, "Would you like to have dinner with me tonight?"

The two handlers looked at each other and spewed out laughter.

Looking at Prescott Susan said, "I'd love to Frank (*Prescott*)," as she climbed up the ladder.

The handlers continued snickering not bothering to make a note of this breach of the rules.

They figured this could count as a scientific breakthrough: One geek asking another for a date.

Prescott kept flirting with Susan as they worked. He walked over to her, and pretending to reference one of the controls on the helm control panel, handed her a small piece of paper with his phone number and address on it.

The fact that Susan had a scrap of paper ready for him was a good sign.

One of the handlers proceeded to walk closer as Prescott pushed the paper into the right cuff of his white lab coat.

Susan kept hoping Prescott was for real.

Prescott, meanwhile, had a pang of guilt. She was after all a nice lady.

It had been a huge gamble and it seemed to be working. He could move forward with 'The Plan'.

Prescott was at a fancy restaurant with Susan. The date was turning out to be stellar for Susan and she couldn't understand why. Susan found Frank (*Prescott*) mysterious and desirable in an intangible way.

Susan couldn't shake the feeling that somehow Frank (*Prescott*) was able to read her mind and she found that irresistible.

Prescott's plan was to use key words in progression using covert reverse hypnosis. Prescott executed flawlessly during their conversation, the hors d'oeuvres and the main course.

Just as Susan was about to take a bite of her lobster Prescott said the post-hypnotic cue words, "Frank is a Bad Boy."

Susan put down her fork and stared directly at Prescott blankly.

Prescott knew this is where things could be dicey if the handlers were to actually hear this part of their conversation. Prescott hoped the handlers weren't trained in lip reading.

Prescott leaned forward and took Susan's hand for the benefit of any handler who might be watching.

Prescott began speaking as softly as he could to Susan while still able to be heard by her.

Turning his head slightly toward the wall next to their corner booth, for which he'd paid the head waiter a hefty bribe, along with another bribe to keep the booth next to theirs empty, Prescott began talking to Susan.

"When you are chosen to be a pilot for the test flight you will hear in your mind 'Frank is a Bad Boy' and provide Frank (*Prescott*) with all of the data and notes you have accumulated on gravity propulsion and all translation documents you have in your possession. Then you will get in your car and drive to Roswell, New Mexico. You will not tell anyone. You will not answer your phone and you will refuse to identify yourself to anyone. Do you understand?"

Susan shook her head up and down indicating she understood. That wasn't good enough for Prescott.

"Tell me yes you understand. Please say it."

Susan mechanically said, "Yes, I understand."

She was a zombie. Prescott felt bad, but this had to be done, or the rest was impossible.

He repeated what he had just told her.

Susan mechanically said again, "Yes, I understand."

"When I say the cue words, you will wake up and you will not remember anything we discussed here."

Prescott said the words.

"Frank is a Bad Boy," Prescott said.

Susan shook her head as if momentarily startled. Prescott eased his hand away from hers and leaned back for the benefit of the handlers.

Susan looked down at her plate wondering what she had last taken a bite of.

Susan realized Frank (Prescott) was a fascinating young man. She was thinking she was in love with him for reasons that were murky. Had she been daydreaming?

The next day Colonel Smith was in his office with the two handlers who had been at the restaurant the night before. They were all laughing as they discussed the two nerds on a date.

"You mean to tell me that last night Frank (*Prescott*) took Susan to a high-class restaurant in Vegas?"

"Yeah, he slipped the maître d' three C-notes to get a corner booth and keep the next booth empty."

"Wow," the Colonel said. "Sounds like true love, or lust at least."

"That's right Colonel," the handlers both confirmed. "That's why we didn't keep any notes. We could barely keep from laughing out loud when we were there."

"The guy was sweet-talking her so much she was like in a trance." Little did they know that Susan really was.

"He's a smooth operator Colonel."

"This is a first," Colonel Smith said, regaining his composure.

"You won't write us up on this, please sir?"

Colonel Smith pondered the situation.

"No, I won't write you up. Let it go. I see no harm in it. Just keep an eye on them."

"Yes sir," the two handlers said as they left his office.

As he thought about this tête-à-tête just described, Colonel Smith chuckled to himself.

"Well, I only hope you didn't enjoy yourself too much on your date with Susan last night," Priscilla said to Prescott only half kidding as they were having one of their phone chats.

"The plan went flawlessly. The post-hypnosis cue words worked."

"What were they again?" Priscilla asked.

"Frank is a Bad Boy," Prescott said.

"Good choice of words, Pres. You are. If all this post-hypnotic suggestion jazz works, Susan will give you all the scoop we need to steal and fly the saucer. Then she will get in her car and drive to Roswell, New Mexico. You instructed her not to tell anyone, not to answer her phone and she will refuse to provide identification to anyone."

"As you said if it all works," he replied.

"And there is no chance it won't work?" she wanted to confirm.

"Let's not go there. You and me Pris. We're gonna steal a flying saucer."

"I'm sure you've already figured the odds that you'll be the pilot on this flight, but does it really matter who drives the stolen car? Just as long as we can hotwire it, right?" she asked.

"Right. It's unbelievable that you found a way to convert the 115 to stable antimatter. How did you do it again? Give me the five-cent version."

"Colonel Smith and everyone else understands the anti-matter reactor in the saucer is designed to convert element 115 into a one hundred percent conversion of matter to energy.

What they don't know is that I've been able to isolate 115 and learned how they manipulate it. I'll explain how I discovered it later. It would take me at least an hour to go over the math and chemistry with you on the phone."

"Please spare me," Prescott petitioned.

She continued.

"Colonel Smith and the handlers now believe we must have Earth's synthesized Element 115 for the anti-matter annihilation reaction. They think I've found out how to increase 115's half-life to four minutes, which would be enough time to create enough antimatter fuel to go to the moon and back for the warp drive flight test.

What they don't know is that it's all the same. The alien's 115 and Earth's 115 are all the same. I've just figured out the aliens' trick. That'll be my claim to fame, if we aren't both lined up on a wall and shot when we return. If we return.

What I don't get is why they haven't figured out after all these years since 1947 and Roswell the trick I just did. They still have blinders on, I suppose."

"Well, if we pull this off as planned, we'll be on our way to Zeta 2 before they find out, or we'll both in dire straits," Prescott said stoically. "That's an understatement."

"I don't know how much longer I can keep up this façade with Colonel Smith and those other guys much longer," Priscilla said in a low whisper.

"I said it before. You're a sly girl. Have some faith in your slyness."

He hoped Susan's hypnosis wouldn't wear off somehow. Unknown to him, the handlers watching that night at the restaurant saw it as just the impulsive youthful lark he had planned it to look like.

Luck would be an important factor in this ruse with Susan.

They had a brief discussion about using suspended animation during the flight and that was quickly dismissed. Even if they knew how to place themselves in suspended animation, how would they unsuspend or unfreeze themselves?

"We need finalize how we're going to provision the saucer with supplies. How long did you estimate it will take us to get to Zeta 2?" Priscilla asked.

Prescott had done some calculations. He and Susan had managed to figure out the different Grey warp speed factors from the translation notes.

"I believe it will take anywhere from one to two months depending on how much we bend spacetime. I think we could push the amplifiers safely to get us there in about six weeks.

The slower we go, the more provisions we need to take, and I don't think I have enough Leave It to Beaver reruns to last longer than that."

"Leave It to who? Beaver? What are you talking about?" Priscilla asked, thinking she'd misunderstood what he'd said.

"Never mind," Prescott replied.

He continued.

"I believe we have three optimal warp cruising speed options. We need to determine if we wish to do one warp speed and keep it constant. I've learned a lot from Susan on gravity propulsion and will continue to glean as much data as I can from her. I won't digress."

"Please don't," she implored. "If you digress like I do I don't want to hear it."

Prescott laughed at her as well as at himself knowing they were both prone to over explaining things.

He continued again.

"At Warp 4 using the amount of gravity wave that will be needed using the projected antimatter consumption numbers you've given me it will take us 4.55 months to travel the 39.24 light years to Serpo orbiting Zeta 2 Reticuli.

Warp 5 will take 2.16 months. Warp 6 will take 1.18 months, or 4.72 weeks, or 36.56 days.

I'm thinking statistically the sweet spot is Warp 5, but if we wanted to accept some risk Warp 6 would save us a month in travel time."

She had an immediate response.

"Since we're already taking an enormous risk, I vote for Warp 6."

Priscilla thought she could feel Prescott smiling through the phone.

"I agree," he said happy with her choice. "Warp 6 it is."

"This call's getting a little long. Let's wrap it up," she said.

She gave Prescott a general outline to acquire enough supplies for the ten-week round trip.

Then they both said good night and good luck.

The next day Priscilla was in Colonel Smith's office making a sales pitch to him.

"I believe it will be important to have these provisions on board during the test flight. Like you said in the first briefing you made to us that day when the first interstellar flight is made the sleeping quarters and restrooms will not be luxuries, they will be necessities.

I would add having food and drink will be as important as the sleeping quarters and restrooms, if not more so. We don't know how their food oven or replicator works, nor how much water would be available over the long haul.

If the unlikely happens during the test flight such as a reactor failure, or a Warp 1 test malfunction and the two-person crew would become stranded, then they'd need food and water. It's a practical consideration for the November test flight."

Colonel Smith moved his head up and down in agreement embarrassed this problem hadn't been allocated more resources and hadn't been more thoroughly researched.

"I can't argue with your logic Sandra *(Priscilla),*" the Colonel remarked. "I am glad to see you taking the initiative on this problem. What are you proposing?"

Priscilla knew she had Colonel Smith like a fish on a hook, she just needed to reel him in slowly and carefully.

"I would like a special allocation of funds to be used at my discretion to board the saucer with enough provisions to maintain two crewmembers for ten weeks. It's a worst-case scenario, but logically I prefer to plan for the worst and hope for the best. I understand the funds would be subject to audit and oversight and I would be happy to get prior approval for my purchases.

Unless we discover how the Grey's food replicator works, I believe one of the logistical challenges will be to find ways to store food and water for an extended interstellar flight once the flight test has been successful."

Colonel Smith scrutinized the earnest young woman sitting in front of him liking her drive and determination and enthusiasm for the mission.

He pulled out a drawer, removed a paper form and filled in some blank space fields and signed his name.

Colonel Smith reached over his desk and handed the completed form to Priscilla.

"Take this form to Finance down the hall in Room 101. It authorizes you to receive $5,000.00 cash in unmarked bills for food and water purchases. If you need more, let me know. Work with your handler. Let's plan on loading the saucer the day before the test flight. The internal modifications on the restrooms and sleeping quarters will be completed by then."

She kept a poker face despite being ready to explode from joy.

"Acknowledged, sir. Thank you, Colonel Smith," Priscilla said evenly as she left his office and went down the hall to Finance to collect the money.

Colonel Smith leaned back in his chair. He had been contemplating the two pilots who would be going on the test flight and had been discussing it with the handlers. His initial choice had been Frank (*Prescott*) Owens and Susan Jones to pilot the saucer.

He was now leaning toward selecting Frank (*Prescott*) Owens and Sandra (*Priscilla*) Jenkins as the two pilots for the test flight.

Colonel Smith decided Sandra's (*Priscilla's*) final selection as a pilot depended on how well she did in the flight simulation testing. He would be in attendance as an observer.

Colonel Smith decided she had spunk. He admired spunk.

Prescott was heaping praise on Priscilla that night during their nocturnal phone chat.

"Five thousand dollars in unmarked bills! That's fantastic. To make sure I understand you just asked the Colonel for the money and he gave it to you?"

"That's about the size of it," she replied, beaming.

"Let me tell you what I want you to buy for the trip," Prescott said, as he launched into a long list of his favorite comfort and junk foods.

Priscilla went with the handler Jim to a wholesale food store and coordinated the bulk purchase of bottled water, canned food, coffee, healthy food, junk food, soft drinks and coffee. And toilet paper and paper towels.

Two microwaves ovens, two small refrigerators, two toasters, a coffee maker and a water purifier were also purchased at a wholesale outlet store, along with two can openers and enough bowls, glasses, plates and silverware for two. The free energy on the ship would power the appliances.

Portable storage units for canned goods and bottled water were included among the purchases and two 55-gallon trash barrels and 100 large plastic trash bags with twists too.

The provisions were delivered to S4 in an unmarked government big rig truck and wheeled into Hangar 7 by forklift where the Executive Model saucer was stored.

The supplies were staged near the saucer and would be loaded onboard the day before the scheduled test flight.

As Priscilla was about to go to sleep, she realized they hadn't discussed the need for change of clothing and doing laundry during their journey to Zeta 2. They also needed to bring basic first aid with them such as band aids, bandages, ointments and aspirin.

And what about showers? No mention was made during the initial briefing by Colonel Smith about the saucer having showers and bathtubs. What about their personal hygiene and her gynecological needs? They needed to bring deodorant, laundry detergent, sunscreen, et al.

She couldn't go to sleep because her mind was racing. She felt this was important enough to warrant an unscheduled call to Prescott. He thought Priscilla had made a butt-dial call, until she explained the urgency.

They reviewed their options into the wee hours of the morning covering clothing, medical supplies, personal hygiene supplies and bedding.

Priscilla successfully asked Colonel Smith for another $1500, which he granted without further ado.

She was also granted permission to requisition on hand Area 51 supplies.

Prescott and Priscilla were running out of time to do everything they needed to do before the test flight that would take them to the fourth planet called Serpo circling the binary star called Zeta 2 Reticuli.

Chapter 11

Saucer Test Flight

An ad hoc classroom had been setup on the bridge of the Executive Model saucer with Susan as the instructor and Prescott and Priscilla as the students, with Colonel Smith and the handlers sitting in the background.

Prescott and Priscilla were sitting behind the console in chairs squeezed snugly in front of the captain's chair taking notes that had to be turned in to the handlers at the end of the class. All handouts Susan was giving out had to be turned in as well.

Susan was finishing up her lecture using a pointer touching various locations on the helm and navigation console panels.

"To recap and summarize, helm and navigation are both on the control panel on the front referred to collectively as the conn. Looking out from the captain's chair helm is on your left and navigation is on your right."

Susan walked toward the conn standing behind it using her pointer as she spoke.

"This helm control is maneuvering thrusters. This one is warp drive. You'll notice here where it's lit up showing the numbers they use for warp 1 through 9. The handout I gave you correlates their numbers with our numbers.

This navigation control is plotting courses and making course corrections. It's a logical design as we discussed in detail earlier. Please refer to the handout I provided for corresponding settings using our references.

Unless you have any questions, I won't go over the captain's chair, the first officer's chair and weapons control in the rear again.

There isn't a specific section devoted to what we could call main engineering. Main engineering seems to be an integrated and shared responsibility of the captain and first officer. My take is the Greys were all adept at engineering skills as a given."

Susan stepped back and circled around standing next to Prescott and Priscilla. Colonel Smith was standing in the front facing them.

"I am going to randomly draw names from my hat to determine the order in which you take your flight simulator exams. As you know, these exams will be used as an important part of your fitness determination to be one of two pilots selected for the warp drive test flight to the moon and back. All of you are qualified, but we can only send two of you."

The handlers had their video recorders ready to record the flight simulator exams.

Colonel Smith was going to be the test proctor, even though Susan designed the test and knew more about the propulsion guidance system and the conn than anyone else. Susan had been keeping him briefed on a daily basis and he had rehearsed his role as test proctor.

Colonel Smith held up three separate slips of paper showing Prescott, Priscilla and Susan that each of their names was listed on one slip. He removed his hat, folded the slips of paper for all to see and placed them in his hat.

Colonel Smith covered his eyes as he reached down and removed a slip. He put on his glasses and looked out at Prescott, Priscilla and Susan. "Susan Jones!" he called out.

Prescott and Priscilla were escorted out of the ship by one of the handlers and taken outside to a holding area that had been set up with a card table and chairs and sodas and sandwiches.

Prescott and Priscilla sat down across from each other and began blinking to each other in Morse Code. A handler was walking around in circles in the background talking on his radio.

"*If Susan third?*" Priscilla blinked.

"*Unlikely,*" Prescott blinked back.

"*Will throw,*" Priscilla blinked.

"*Ok,*" Prescott blinked back.

After twenty minutes Colonel Smith, Susan and the other handler emerged from the saucer. Susan was escorted away.

Colonel Smith came over to the card table and took a chair. He removed his hat, showed Prescott and Priscilla the slips of paper with their names on them, folded them and placed them in his hat. He then covered his eyes as he reached down and removed a slip.

"Sandra (*Priscilla*) Jenkins!" Colonel Smith said.

Priscilla followed the Colonel and a handler into the saucer for her flight simulator exam.

Twenty minutes later Priscilla and Colonel Smith exited the saucer. Colonel Smith gestured for Prescott to come inside as Priscilla took a seat at the card table as Susan joined her.

Colonel Smith stuck his head out of the open door of the saucer and shouted to Priscilla and Susan, "Come inside!"

Priscilla and Susan followed by a handler hustled inside the saucer and joined Prescott, who was standing behind the conn.

Colonel Smith positioned himself in front of the conn, put on his glasses and looked at the exam results he had tabulated on a sheet of paper.

"These are the results of the flight simulator exams," he began.

"Frank (*Prescott*) Owens, 94.

Sandra (*Priscilla*) Jenkins, 83.

Susan Jones, 81."

Priscilla was standing in disbelief. She had knowingly answered four questions incorrectly and had pretended to delay keying in a flight course correction. How could Susan come in third? Susan designed the test and was the instructor on the helm and navigation console panels. She must have choked.

Prescott was trying to comprehend while already planning corrective actions. Since Susan didn't hear that she'd been selected as a pilot the post-hypnosis cue words 'Frank is a Bad Boy' weren't triggered in her subconscious and were now defunct.

She wouldn't be driving to Roswell and wouldn't be turning over her gravity propulsion guidance notes and documentation and the translation documents that were vital for Prescott and Priscilla to have for their journey to Zeta 2.

"You all did well and I am proud of all of you," Colonel Smith said, privately happy that Sandra (*Priscilla*) was one of the two pilots. "Frank (*Prescott*) and Sandra (*Priscilla*), you will be the pilots for the warp test flight to the moon. I'm sorry Susan you just missed the cut."

Susan graciously gave Prescott and Priscilla congratulations shaking their hands. Susan whispered in Prescott's ear, "I wish it would have been you and me."

Prescott nodded in surrogate sympathy to Susan looking over at Priscilla, who blinked out a message.

"*I call PM.*"

"Any ideas?" Priscilla said as Prescott picked up his phone.

"Yes," he replied. "To think I had estimated there was a seventy-one percent chance Susan would be chosen as a pilot. I've never been that far off the mark. You even cheated on the test to your detriment and Susan still came in third.

Another thing. It wasn't necessary for me to have placed in Susan's mind the suggestion when she heard she'd been selected as one of the two pilots for the test flight the cue words 'Frank is a Bad Boy' would kick in.

I could have used another pretext besides her selection as one of the test pilots to have her give us the translation and propulsion documents and then drive to Roswell, New Mexico. To use an engineering analogy, I overengineered my covert reverse hypnosis approach with her."

"Don't badger yourself on what you should have done," she counseled. "Find a solution asap. If it makes you feel any better, I thought Susan was a shoe-in to be selected too."

"I'm going to have to put Susan under hypnosis again to restore her suppressed memories from amnesia on the original 'Frank is a Bad Boy' suggestion. I'll condition her to give us her gravity propulsion notes with the documentation backup she cross-referenced and all the translation documents."

Priscilla wasn't understanding.

"You're the person with the master's in psychology and I defer to your expertise, but I'm not following you. Why can't you just give her the suggestion that on your cue words she'll just hand over the gravity propulsion and translation documents she has, or more correctly stated, she has access to. I doubt she's got the translation documents lying around her living room."

"It's not as straightforward and simple as that Pris," he replied. "I've got to handle this carefully because she still has repressed memories. The approach I used on her is novel and I've not heard or read of my particular hypnosis technique ever being used before.

I'm in uncharted waters because I made Susan fall in love with me."

"You did, did you?" Priscilla said, slightly annoyed despite herself.

"I had to honey," he replied.

"I know you did. How many dates have you had with Susan so far?"

"Three."

Prescott continued.

"I'm going to condition her so when I provide her with the new cue words 'Frank is a Good Boy' her previous repressed memory about providing us with the gravity propulsion guidance notes and associated backup and the translation documents will be brought to her conscious mind unconsciously.

I think she should still drive to Roswell because it will add to the general confusion at Area 51 when we depart.

I've got to handle it carefully, because from what I've been able to find out from Susan the translation documents and her gravity propulsion guidance notes are kept in a safe in Colonel Smith's office. She doesn't have the combination to the safe, so the timing has to be well thought out. It must be done the day we are scheduled to leave without detection.

Usually the procedure is for her to request the translation documents from Colonel Smith and return them by the end of the day. You know Colonel Smith and what a stickler he is for following procedure."

"I don't know anything about hypnosis and not much about psychology either. I know you'll do the right thing," Priscilla said to bolster his confidence.

He had an afterthought.

"Talking about Colonel Smith and his being a stickler for procedure, I'm surprised there hasn't been any blowback from the first date I had with Susan at that upscale restaurant in Las Vegas and the two other dates we've had. That's against procedure and there are supposed to be severe penalties for violating it.

I did calculate there was an eight-two percent probability my taking Susan out to dinner would be written off by them as an impulse. There's no question we're under surveillance on our dates. Still, I'm surprised nobody has said anything.

Pris, luck has been with us so far in many ways. Believe it or not, I can't calculate the odds, but I know this lucky trend can't last."

She began giggling.

"They probably find it funny that you are dating Susan. It must be a laugh factory in Colonel Smith's office when he's alone in there with the handlers."

Prescott joined Priscilla's snickering.

"I know you told me you almost became a computer science major at Caltech and are a geek. Are you a good computer hacker?" he asked her.

"I can do it. Why?" she wanted to know.

"We've got to cover our tracks the night of our flight. We need a diversion that the security guard will see and believe. Here's my plan."

"Hold that thought," Priscilla said as she went to the kitchen and took a container of salsa and dipping tortilla chips and brought them back into her living room.

Priscilla dipped a chip relishing telling Prescott important news she'd been saving as a surprise.

"I'm back. Before you tell me your plan, today I was able to determine the radio frequency of the remote that Colonel Smith uses to open the saucer. It wasn't easy. I duplicated it."

"Awesome!" Prescott replied. "I know we've discussing that as part of our to do punch list. That's critical. Without the frequency we can't open the saucer hatch door. How did you pull that off?"

"I used my iPhone," Priscilla proudly replied. "I asked Colonel Smith I needed to go into the ship today and when he pointed his remote at it, I was able to get the frequency. I was able to do a sneak verification test using my iPhone without anyone being the wiser. It worked."

Prescott laughed thinking of that scene.

"You are special," he said. "Your iPhone is now a remote control to open the hatch door of a flying saucer too. I know there's more to it than that, but we've got a lot to go over tonight. You can tell me when we are in route to Zeta 2."

Three days later Prescott was back at the same fancy restaurant with Susan again they had dined at on their first date. He had called ahead and made a reservation. This time he visited the restaurant ahead of time securing the same corner booth he and Susan had shared after employing some spreading around money.

Prescott knew he was walking on a fault line because it had been made abundantly clear to him that consummation of their relationship was on Susan's radar screen. He decided to incorporate that concern into the hypnosis he would place Susan under tonight.

The restaurant was humming and the joint was jumping providing excellent cover noise.

The waiter brought their first course. Susan took the bottle of red wine and topped off Prescott's glass.

"You're not drinking much wine, Frank (*Prescott*)," Susan said, as he did a quick look around.

Prescott picked up his wine glass and angled it slightly toward Susan. "I toast the most beautiful woman in the world."

Susan shuddered in delight and raised her wine glass touching Prescott's glass as he launched into his covert hypnosis technique, guiding an unsuspecting Susan down the primrose path.

Just as Susan was about to take a bite of her Coq au Vin, Prescott said the hypnosis cue words, "Frank is a Good Boy."

Susan put down her fork and stared at Prescott blankly.

Prescott knew that just like last time this is where things could be vulnerable if the handlers would hear this part of their conversation. Prescott had already turned his face toward the wall to preclude lip reading.

Using the method acting approach Prescott leaned forward and took Susan's hand for the benefit of the handlers who were watching.

"On the day before the test flight when we are at Area 51, I will tell you the words 'Frank is a Good Boy' and you will ask Colonel Smith for all of the translation documents he keeps in his safe.

You will tell Colonel Smith you need to double check some alien Grey language to English translations of the navigation console because you want to be absolutely sure that there are no mistranslations before the test flight.

You will tell Colonel Smith you will return the documents to him at 1000 hours the next day. You will also give me any documentation and notes you have on gravity propulsion guidance. Do you understand?"

Susan shook her head up and down indicating she understood. Just as it was on their previous date at this restaurant it wasn't good enough for Prescott.

"Tell me yes you understand. Please say it."

Susan mechanically said, "Yes, I understand."

"After you give me all of the translation and gravity propulsion guidance documents and notes you have in your possession you will get in your car and drive to Roswell, New Mexico. You will not tell anyone. You will not answer your phone and you will refuse to identify yourself to anyone. Do you understand?"

Susan mechanically said, "Yes, I understand."

"You will also lose any desire that you may have for me sexual or otherwise. You are not in love with me. Again, you will also lose any desire you may have for me sexual or otherwise. You are not in love with me. Do you understand?"

Susan mechanically said, "Yes, I understand."

"When I say the cue words, you will wake up and you will not remember anything we discussed here. The next time you hear the cue words will be at Area 51 and you will comply with the instructions you have been given. Do you understand?"

Susan mechanically said, "Yes, I understand."

Prescott was pensive as he was about to bring Susan out of her trance using the same hypnotic cue words.

"Frank is a Good Boy," Prescott said.

Susan found herself shaking her head and her mind was muddled. Prescott took his hand away from hers and stared at her for the benefit of the handlers.

Susan realized Frank (*Prescott*) was a smart young man, but was shocked she no longer considered him to be alluring and appealing. What had caused that?

All she wanted to do now was go home alone. How could she have fallen in love with him?

The next day Colonel Smith was in his office laughing along with the two handlers who had monitored Prescott and Susan at the restaurant.

He always enjoyed the periodic updates his handlers gave him on Frank (*Prescott*) and Susan. They livened up his day.

"You're saying that Frank (*Prescott*) took Susan back to that same expensive restaurant in Las Vegas?" Colonel Smith inquired.

"Yes. When we walked in, Frank (Prescott) and Susan were already sitting at the same corner booth they'd sat at last time. He'd phoned ahead and made a reservation."

Colonel Smith leaned back in his chair.

"Did they sleep together?" he asked, eagerly awaiting an update on that possibility.

The handlers shook their heads no.

"Colonel, that is what's interesting," one of the handlers said. "At the restaurant the kid was really sweet-talking Susan like he did the last time they were there and he was stroking her hand the same way. But," the handler's voice trailed off.

"But what?" Colonel Smith wanted to know.

"But something was too similar, too rehearsed."

"Similar? Rehearsed? What the hell do you mean by that?" Colonel Smith urgently asked, alarm bells beginning to go off in his mind.

He was getting his blood up and quickly stood up.

"Why in the hell didn't you guys tell me this already? Similar? Rehearsed? Explain what you mean."

The handler who spoke first remained quiet. The other handler spoke instead.

"I think what Bob means is Susan was saying the same thing she did the last time they were at the restaurant 'Yes, I understand'. Susan had the same blank look on her face just like the last time she and the kid were at the restaurant."

Colonel Smith eased himself back down in his chair.

"Bob, Jim I'm sorry for yelling at you. I'm really yelling at myself for allowing this situation between Frank (*Prescott*) and Susan to have gone on for as long as it has. Bring me the personnel files on Frank and Susan. I may ask you to do supplementary investigations."

Colonel Smith straightened up in his chair.

"As soon as you leave my office let them both know verbally their relationship has officially come to an end. Tell them they are to never see one another again except for working here at Sector 4. From this moment on they are under the tightest surveillance. If you need additional resources advise me and I will arrange it."

"Yes sir," the two handlers said as they left his office.

Colonel Smith realized the idea of the kid dating Susan wasn't so funny after all.

Priscilla could tell Prescott was upset as they began their now nightly telephone conversation.

"Ok, slow down. What happened exactly?" she wanted to know.

"Today Bob, you know, one of the handlers bluntly told me I was not to see Susan any longer under no circumstances except as necessary at work," he replied.

Priscilla wanted to be sure she understood the context.

"And this is a bad thing because?"

"Because this is the day after Susan and I had dinner at the restaurant last night. I know we were under surveillance. They let the first date at the restaurant pass, then the two other dates where we went to a movie and the third date where we went to a comedy club and they said nothing about that. We were under surveillance then too. I take her back to the same restaurant and the next day suddenly we can't see each other anymore other than at work."

"Well Pres, personally I'm glad you've been banned from seeing Susan she's not your type. But I see your point. You're concerned about what it could mean."

"Yes. To me it's ominous because they may have picked up something last night. Bob and Jim are intelligent. Naturally they would be if they are working at Area 51. Something they observed last night was a trigger."

"Did you do anything out of the ordinary?" she wanted to know, beginning to see the potential seriousness of the situation.

"No. That's it. I did the same thing last night I did the first time I was at the restaurant with Susan when I hypnotized her."

He paused as a light bulb went on in his brain.

"That's it! They saw that Susan was hypnotized. They may not have known she was under hypnosis, but they know something similar happened last night that happened during our first date.

My bad! I had her say the same words 'Yes, I understand' last night just like the first time at the restaurant. I bet they read her lips and that tipped them off. That, plus the look on her face, which was a blank stare. Why didn't I think of that?"

"Don't go tearing yourself up inside," Priscilla said, trying to shore up Prescott's morale. "We're still planning to leave the day after tomorrow in the evening, correct? Based on what we discussed the other night? I committed it all to memory. You'll give Susan the cue words 'Frank is a Good Boy' in the late morning or early afternoon before we leave, correct?"

"Correct," he said, feeling insecure and unsure of himself.

She decided to play devil's advocate to argue for leaving the day of the scheduled test flight.

"Why don't we wait until Thursday when the test flight is scheduled?" Priscilla asked Prescott wanting to be sure they were making the most informed decision.

"Haven't we gone over this already?" he asked her without receiving an answer.

"First of all, in my opinion, it has become increasingly clear to me that having the translation documents and Susan's notes on gravity guidance propulsion with her cross-referenced documentation backup is no longer a luxury, but a necessity. It could mean the difference between life and death.

I have determined if we try to acquire the documents on the day of the flight scheduled for 1100 hours our odds will decrease exponentially that we will be able to obtain them. Don't ask me to itemize the reasons just trust me.

Second of all, your new handler in the chemistry lab Roger is getting suspicious about your lie of finding a four-minute window of stable antimatter from Element 115, right? Isn't that what you've been telling me?" Prescott asked Priscilla pointedly.

"True," she admitted. "I wouldn't use the word suspicious. Roger's more like confused at this point. He thinks I'm telling the truth and he thinks he's not catching on. I've managed to cover my tracks, but I won't be able to do so indefinitely. He's a good chemist. Eventually he'll go to Colonel Smith and the gig will be up."

"I rest my case," he declared. "We must depart on Wednesday. We will have the element of surprise on our side. I know what you're thinking our plan depends on almost nothing going wrong and it's very risky. If we find ourselves stranded in space a dozen light years from Earth because something's gone wrong with the reactor or the propulsion that we can't fix because we don't have the translation documents and Susan's personal notes, then we'll wish we'd left a day earlier."

"I withdraw my suggestion," Priscilla said.

"We've only got two more days to go until Wednesday," he said. "Tomorrow Colonel Smith will give us a tour of the completed saucer modifications. We've come up with a brilliant departure plan. It's going to work. Two more days is all we need."

"That and lots of luck," she added, knowing how often he said luck was an important factor.

Priscilla had a feeling Prescott wasn't as confident as he sounded.

The next day Prescott, Priscilla and Susan were gathered together in Hangar 7 to observe the modifications that were being made to the Executive Model saucer.

The two handlers Bob and Jim were keeping a close eye on Prescott and Susan watching their every move and emotion. They noticed Susan's body language indicated her outward display of passion for Frank (*Prescott*) had cooled since the last date she had with Frank (*Prescott*) at the restaurant. Frank (*Prescott*) was inscrutable as always, except when he was pitching woo to Susan at the restaurant.

The handlers were beginning to wonder if Frank (*Prescott*) had ever taken acting lessons and decided to look into it.

Standing next to the ramp Colonel Smith was making a brief statement before they all entered the saucer for an inspection tour.

"Workers are inside cleaning up. Everything is done. Let's check it out."

Colonel Smith led them in. Prescott, Priscilla and Susan then entered, followed by Bob and Jim.

He walked the group down the corridor into the restroom.

"We were able to enlarge the toilet and urinal without disturbing the auto-flush feature. The sinks were enlarged too."

They exited the restroom and entered one of the two bedrooms.

"The metallurgical team was able to remove the fixed furniture and bunks in the bedrooms. The metallurgical team is made up of wizards. Don't ask me how they did it. We bought two new bunks beds, two desks and four chairs at a local discount furniture outlet. The bunk beds barely fit inside the bedrooms, but humans can comfortably sit in the chairs and sleep in the beds."

As they exited the bedroom Colonel Smith pointed to the new standard sized dining table with four chairs placed around it.

"If you need to eat a sit-down meal on the saucer you can do it now. The new dining room table and chairs crowd things a little, but it's not too bad. The retractable bed in sick bay was left as it is. The original bunk beds and dining room table and desks and chairs have been removed and placed in storage in Hangar 7. The original helm and navigation chairs are being kept in storage on the bridge.

As you all have already noticed by working in the saucer the inside lighting is variable and is on a 15-hour cycle, which we believe correlates to the length of their day and night based on their planet's rotation around their star Zeta 2 Reticuli. However, this cycle may have nothing to do with the length of their day and night, if they have a night. We don't know."

They walked down the corridor and entered the bridge.

"As you can see, we were able to remove the two fixed chairs at the helm and navigation stations and replace them with normal sized chairs.

There is still the problem of being able to put your legs underneath the conn. You three should be able to it better than most because frankly you three are a little smaller on average than many people."

Colonel Smith walked over to the captain's chair.

"At Susan's recommendation we decided not to tamper with the captain's chair because of that reason meaning the tie in of command buttons on the captain's chair to certain system-wide functions.

If this craft ever went on an interstellar flight, the actual captain of that mission would have to improvise as needed using a regular sized chair possible directly in front. However, if one of you was the captain you might be able to squeeze into the chair."

Priscilla and Prescott exchanged quick glances.

The Colonel continued.

"The first officer's chair doesn't have any built-in command buttons, but it has a monitor screen and some control buttons. The first officer's station appears to be primarily for status and for providing the captain with ship wide recommendations. The third chair is only a chair.

The work station behind those three chairs has conclusively identified as weapons control.

Thanks to the hard work of Frank (*Prescott*) and Susan we know two of the gravity amplifiers double as weapons that bleed off antimatter into a focused photon beam. Frank (*Prescott*) and Susan were able to verify this using the translation documents.

Either there are threats to the Greys, or the Greys perceive there are threats against them.

No modifications were made to the bottom level. Let me take this opportunity to acknowledge the superb work done by Sandra (*Priscilla*) in discovering how to extend the half-life of Element 115 to four minutes that will provide enough antimatter for the fuel for the warp drive test to the moon and back."

Colonel Smith began clapping as did Prescott and Susan. Priscilla looked at Prescott who had a wry look on his face. Priscilla felt uneasy and vulnerable as she managed a weak smile.

"Great job Sandra (*Priscilla*) we owe you for that one," the Colonel concluded. "One more thing. Regarding all of the food and water and other supplies staged outside the saucer that was Sandra's (*Priscilla's*) idea. There are enough supplies to sustain a crew of two for approximately ten weeks if my calculations are correct.

I believe it was an excellent idea to have these supplies on board for the warp drive test. During actual interstellar journeys such levels of supplies will be needed. Sandra (*Priscilla*), the supplies will be loaded on board tomorrow."

Colonel Smith began clapping again as did Prescott and Susan.

He had a final word.

"In two days, Thursday to exact, our pilots Frank (*Prescott*) and Sandra (*Priscilla*) will pilot the warp drive test to the moon. We are going through extensive subterfuge to keep anyone who might be listening meaning the Russians, the Chinese, the Europeans the whole damn world from finding out about this vital mission. If it works, then the balance of power will dramatically shift in our favor. I know you are all patriots. The country is depending on you Frank (*Prescott*) and Sandra (*Priscilla*)."

For the third time Colonel Smith broke into applause as did Susan and the two handlers. Despite Susan's loss of interest in Frank (*Prescott*) romantically she still respected his tremendous knowledge of physics.

Prescott and Priscilla were feeling uncomfortable and guilty as the clapping went on and on fidgeting and giving each other furtive glances as the clapping went on and on knowing all the accolades were actually lauding them for the very abilities that would enable them to hijack the saucer and take them on a journey to the Grey's home planet known as Serpo circling the binary star known as Zeta 2 Reticuli.

They had grimly discussed several times on the phone the possibility that if their plan were uncovered, or if they were unsuccessful, they would face the death penalty.

They weren't traitors. They were visionaries.

The night before their departure Prescott and Priscilla had a long phone discussion going over all details of their plan to steal the saucer. Each one of them recited the plan step by step to the other for four times. Their photographic memories remembered every detail.

They had a long discussion about aborting and backing out weighing the pros and cons and finally convincing themselves though it might be immoral and though it might be illegal they were moving ahead.

Backing out was NOT an option. The pros and cons were now irrelevant. They were going to Zeta and their reason was simple. They knew they could do it.

They also broached the possibility that something could go wrong as they left Earth's atmosphere, or while they were in route to Zeta 2. There were no guarantees. If they got stranded, they had ten weeks of supplies. After that, even if they had water they would starve to death unless they could figure out how the Grey's food replicators worked. Or they would die of thirst, unless the Grey's water supply kept them going.

Prescott and Priscilla concluded they had burned their bridges and there was no looking back. There was only one way to go. Up.

It was only a matter of time before Colonel Smith found out she had lied about creating a stable antimatter half-life for four minutes from Element 115.

It was only a matter of time before Colonel Smith would figure out Susan had been hypnotized by him turning her into an unwilling pawn in a plot to steal a government owned alien-built spaceship that had been assigned the highest security clearance classification.

Prescott determined the odds were one hundred percent these two crimes would be uncovered within a week at most. More realistically, Prescott determined it could be in three days or less.

Prescott and Priscilla decided if push came to shove Prescott would abandon his plan to obtain the translations from Susan. It could be fatal, but at this point they might have to take that risk.

Nervous and tired, they both went to bed filled with apprehension and foreboding.

Tomorrow could be their last day on Earth.

Prescott and Priscilla left their homes as always. Prescott had no doubt he was under heightened surveillance.

They arrived as always at the McCarron airport in Las Vegas to begin their daily commute to Area 51.

During the twenty-minute flight from Las Vegas to Area 51 Prescott and Priscilla were going over the plan step by step mentally rehearsing. They knew one mistake no matter how small could derail their plan and perhaps cost them their lives. This was made clear during their Area 51 onboarding.

As the bus skidded to a halt in front of S4, Prescott looked at Priscilla, noticing her hands were trembling a little. He was wound a bit tight too. He told her about different relaxation techniques trying to make it look like 'Good Morning' small talk.

He knew they needed to be focused while exhibiting a calm demeanor. Business as usual.

Iron will and discipline and luck. Lots of luck.

The first thing Prescott did was make sure that Susan was at work. Prescott got to the saucer full of anxiety because if for whatever reason Susan wasn't at work, he'd have to implement his backup plan, which was a long shot at best.

Colonel Smith needed to be at work today as well because only he had the key to the safe where the translation documents and gravity propulsion guidance notes and related materials were kept.

After checking in with a handler, Prescott entered the saucer and saw Susan going over a list with Colonel Smith. Why was Colonel Smith at the saucer so early? Prescott was happy that both of them were at work today of all days.

Colonel Smith saw him and gave no outward indication he was in any way suspicious.

"Good morning, Frank (*Prescott*)," he said in a friendly manner. "Tomorrow is the big day. How do you feel?"

"Fine, sir. Thank you. Are you here checking the conn?"

"Susan is giving helm and navigation a final once over before tomorrow's flight. I'd like to meet with you and Sandra (*Priscilla*) later today in my office to go over some final agenda items. I'll let you know when."

"Yes sir, Colonel Smith," Prescott said.

Colonel Smith looked at Prescott as if he was scrutinizing him.

"Why don't you take the morning off, Frank (*Prescott*). Go to the canteen, have a leisurely brunch. I want you and Priscilla rested for tomorrow's flight. Have you seen Sandra (*Priscilla*) this morning?"

"Thank you, sir. No sir, I haven't seen Sandra (*Priscilla*)."

Prescott exited the saucer and walked away quickly headed for the canteen as Colonel Smith suggested. Something isn't right, Prescott thought.

Jim, one of the handlers, was walking behind him.

As Prescott walked away, Colonel Smith flagged Bob, the other handler, with an unspoken signal. "Excuse me, Susan, I need to speak with Bob about something. I'll be back in a few minutes."

"Yes sir," Susan said.

Colonel Smith and Bob walked down the corridor to the other side of the saucer and began whispering.

"What did you find in the supplemental background check on Frank (*Prescott*) Owens?"

"He's got a master's degree in Psychology. You know what in?" Bob remarked.

"No, you tell me that's what I'm paying you for," Colonel Smith retorted, out of sorts.

"We knew this already, but it could be significant in retrospect after what Jim and I saw at the restaurant. The kid's psychology master's thesis was in covert reverse hypnosis. I'm saying it could be significant because Jim and I agree Susan wasn't all together both times we saw her with the kid at that restaurant. Let me amend that. She was normal until he began what looked like sweet-talking her as we've told you, then she changed. We didn't really see it until the second time they were at dinner together."

"That 'kid'," Colonel Smith reminded Bob, "Is going to be one of two pilots who take this saucer out for a test run to the moon and back. He may be young, but he's no kid. Now explain to me why you believe his having master's thesis is significant; what was it in again?"

"Covert reverse hypnosis."

"Sounds like a bunch of baloney to me. Explain to me why you and Jim believe his having master's thesis in covert reverse hypnosis is significant?"

"Jim and I think Susan may have been hypnotized. That is, brought into a state of hypnosis. Look at the first word of the title of his thesis. It's the word covert. He also studied method acting at some college for one semester."

"Acting? He doesn't look like the type who'd be into that. You've read his psychological profile. He's a shy person, except when it comes to Susan. That's probably nothing. Why would he hypnotize Susan?" Colonel Smith asked rhetorically. "That's if he did, and I'm not convinced he did, at least not yet. Is it possible that he hypnotized her to get her into bed or something?"

Bob sighed.

"I don't know. If you'd been there, you'd understand. I know it sounds strange and I'll be the first to admit this could be way off base. There's probably nothing to it. Yet Jim and I still have a gut feeling that he wasn't whispering sweet nothings in her ear. Something else was going on, but we can't put our fingers on it. One more observation to report. Susan isn't flirting with the kid anymore – I mean Frank (*Prescott*)."

"You ordered her to break up with him, correct?" Colonel Smith fumed irritably. "Damn right she's not flirting with him anymore. I've got to get back to Susan we're breaking protocol by leaving her alone by the conn. Continue to keep Frank (*Prescott*) under close watch. Anything going on with Sandra (*Priscilla*)?"

"No sir, same old same old with her. This morning she seemed preoccupied. She's in the chemistry lab with Roger. I checked in with her about an hour ago. That's when I noticed she seems nervous this morning."

"Help Jim keep a watch on Frank (*Prescott*). If push comes to shove and I have any doubts no matter how ill founded, I'm replacing Frank (*Prescott*) with Susan on the test flight."

"Yes sir," Bob said as he headed for the canteen.

Prescott was sitting in the canteen nervously finishing his eggs benedict and coffee. Jim was sitting a few tables away eating breakfast and Bob joined him.

Prescott was going over his options.

It was more than obvious to Prescott that he was under heightened surveillance. He was doing a cost-benefit analysis trying to determine if giving Susan the cue word 'Frank is a Good Boy' was worth the risk.

Prescott was beginning to doubt the reasoning he and Priscilla had come up with to steal government property and possibly take it on a wild goose chase to the stars. Based on his training in psychology Prescott was beginning to wonder if he and Priscilla were clinically insane.

They were criminals and no amount of cognitive dissonance could cover that up.

The translation documents and propulsion guidance notes Susan could obtain would be invaluable for the flight to Zeta 2. All emergency instructions were included within the translations and everything the Greys had codified on the helm and navigation was contained in the translations, along with details about many aspects of ship's operations.

Even though Prescott and Priscilla were sure the simulation training they'd receive would suffice, the translations would be like having an insurance policy in the event something bad or unforeseen happened during their flight to Serpo.

Prescott put any thought of aborting the mission and any moral concerns on the back burner and decided to move ahead with the plan. He needed to get the cue words to Susan by 10:00 am. That was only 15 minutes from now. He'd pull the trigger then. Any later would remove the margin for error he'd painstakingly built into the plan.

Prescott walked over to Bob and Jim as nonchalantly as he could.

"Good morning Bob, good morning Jim," Prescott said.

"Good morning," they cautiously replied.

"As you know, the test flight is tomorrow. I need to ask Susan a question about navigation. I was wondering if we could do that before I begin my final flight preparation this afternoon?"

Bob and Jim looked at each other.

Bob slowly said, "I thought Colonel Smith gave you the morning off."

"He did. Yes, he did. I just can't get this confusion I have about inputting course corrections out of my mind. It would be helpful if I got it straightened out."

After a lengthy pause, Bob said, "Sure Frank (*Prescott*). Just let me finish my cereal. Five minutes."

He slowly walked back to his table and waited sensing they were suspicious.

Five minutes later Bob said to Prescott, "Let's go," as Bob and Jim escorted him to the saucer.

He entered the saucer with the two handlers right behind him. Susan was sitting in a regular chair next to the original captain's chair looking at the control buttons.

Flanked by Bob and Jim, Prescott looked at them waiting for permission to speak to Susan. "Go ahead," Jim said.

"Susan, at the navigation station I'm not sure if the course corrections are input left to right or right to left because the Grey's numbering system still causes me some confusion."

"Really?" Susan said in surprise especially since Prescott came in first on the flight simulator exam with a grade of 94. "It's pretty rudimentary."

"I know," he laughed, "But you know how anal I can be. Frank is a Good Boy."

Prescott saw Susan momentarily blank out, then instantly return to consciousness.

Jim cocked his head. "What did you say, Frank (*Prescott*)?"

"Say about what? I asked Susan about course corrections and she's about to show me."

Before Jim could say anything to scribble in shorthand what he thought he heard as part of his transcribing their conversation, Susan began explaining to Prescott the methodology for inputting course corrections.

"Thank you very much Susan. That clears it up for me."

Looking at Bob and Jim, Prescott said, "Now that that's settled, I'll take the rest of the morning off by going to the basketball court. Care to play a game of pick-up?"

"You've never won," Bob laughed. "Sure, I'll play a game of pick-up with you. I'll even let Jim tag team for you. In honor of your test flight tomorrow."

Prescott took a last look at Susan hoping that everything would flow according to plan.

Priscilla was killing time in the lab until takeoff in the saucer.

She knew her fraudulent machinations about finding a way to convert Element 115 to stable antimatter for four minutes were treading on thin ice.

Roger, a chemist handler who'd been with her for the last few days, was studying her daily logs and was beginning to suspect something was amiss with her report conclusions. Roger was contemplating letting Colonel Smith know about his concerns.

Pricilla had managed to bluff her way through several pointed questions Roger had already asked her this morning. Her heart was pounding. She looked at her watch. It was 10:34 am. What was Prescott doing?

According to the plan he should have already given Susan the 'Frank is a Good Boy' cue words setting in motion Susan retrieving all of the gravity propulsion guidance documentation and notes and translation documents.

Roger asked her another question and she had to cover up one lie with another lie. This couldn't go on much longer.

Roger was thinking if he couldn't reconcile Sandra's (*Priscilla's*) calculations with his observations, he would have to inform Colonel Smith.

Priscilla was getting close to the breaking point and was seriously considering rushing to find Prescott to tell him they should abort the mission.

Back in the saucer just after Prescott and the handlers left Susan was double-checking the alien writing on the captain's button panel embedded in the captain's chair. Something isn't meshing, Susan thought, that's not correct.

Susan went over to the navigation panel and did some cross-checking. "That isn't right," she said to herself.

Just at that moment Colonel Smith walked in the bridge.

"Perfect timing sir. I was just going to come see you. I just found what could be a possible anomaly in the translation of the captain's button panel."

"Seriously?" he replied with concern. "I thought you'd checked everything out already. We've already had the flight simulator exams. I'm wondering why this is coming up now."

Susan was feeling embarrassed and didn't understand why she was making this request.

"I apologize sir if I missed anything before. I need to double check some of the English translations of the navigation console because I want to be absolutely sure that there are no mistranslations before the test flight.

I don't think it's a major issue, but in light of the test flight tomorrow I would feel as if I'm betraying the mission if I didn't bring this up."

Colonel Smith studied Susan. She was a dedicated physicist who had jumped over hundreds of candidates, thousands actually, to get where she is. Although she'd inexplicably succumbed to Frank (*Prescott*) for whatever reason she still seemed solid and dedicated.

Colonel Smith decided the idea that Susan had been hypnotized Frank (*Prescott*) to be ridiculous. Just because Frank had effectively hit on her didn't mean she'd been hypnotized by him.

"What do you need Susan?" Colonel Smith asked.

"All of the translation documents including my own gravity guidance propulsion notes. I want to be thorough and comprehensive. It's important considering the pending flight test tomorrow."

She looked forthright and sincere.

"Alright," Colonel Smith finally said. "How long will you need them?"

"I should be able to return them tomorrow at 1000 hours. I'll leave them lying in a chair on the bridge overnight if that is acceptable."

Colonel Smith almost said no, then decided under the circumstances that was acceptable.

"Agreed," Colonel Smith said. He had a hundred things on his mind.

Susan followed Colonel Smith to his office. He went to what looked like a smooth wall surface in the corner of his office and inserted a key opening a large wall safe full of documents.

"Ok, let me see where they are," the Colonel muttered as he rifled through several sets of documents. One large binder was lying in the safe. "Here they are," Colonel Smith said.

Colonel Smith removed the large binder containing the translation documents and Susan's gravity propulsion documentation and notes from the safe. He took out a clip board with a ledger that was also in the safe and noted the date and time the documents were being removed and the description of the documents. He also signed both line items one for each set of documents.

He handed the clipboard to Susan who dutifully signed both line items. Colonel Smith handed the master binder containing all of it to Susan.

"Thank you, Colonel Smith. I'll return them tomorrow at 1000 hours."

"Had enough?" Bob the handler said, slightly winded. "How about one more game?" Jim the other handler said. "How about it, Frank (*Prescott*)?"

"No thanks, Jim," Prescott said. "Bob beat us two games straight and that's enough humiliation for one day. I need to prep myself for tomorrow's flight."

Bob and Jim extended their hands to Prescott.

"Best of luck tomorrow, Frank (*Prescott*)," Bob said sincerely.

"Thank you," Prescott replied.

He checked the time. It was 11:05 am.

As he'd hoped, Bob and Jim walked to the gym shower. Prescott tensely waited expecting them to turn around and tell him to come with them and breathed a sigh of relief as he watched them enter the sauna and shower room and disappear inside. If they hadn't done that, he would have had to resort to his shaky backup plan.

Prescott knew by Area 51 regulations he was to be accompanied at all times by at least one handler.

The day to day interactions Prescott and Priscilla had with the handlers had softened that approach to a certain extent.

Prescott knew Bob and Jim were suspicious and they had probably spied on him and Susan in disguise at the restaurant. He wondered what they had been thinking as they had observed what appeared to be his hitting on Susan. They must have found it comical. They must have determined that something was up that second time at the restaurant. That's probably why Bob had told him he was prohibited from seeing Susan outside of work.

Prescott wiped his face with a towel. He wasn't too sweaty and had fumbled and stumbled around playing the uncoordinated nerd. Prescott didn't have to do much acting to accomplish that goal. He'd allowed Jim do most of the heavy lifting during the game, who'd worked up an actual sweat. Besides Bob and Jim had a height advantage over him when they were playing basketball together.

Prescott closed his eyes and psyched himself up. This was for all the marbles.

While he and Priscilla could launch without the translation documents and gravity propulsion documentation and notes, having them could mean the difference between life and death in the dark icy cold of space. There were hundreds of unknown variables that could come into play. Prescott was at a loss to predict them all and opted not to try.

Prescott hurried to the saucer before Bob and Jim finished their showers and before any other handler saw him walking around Area 51 by his lonesome.

Prescott slowly entered the saucer and briefly walked down the corridor and onto the bridge. There she was. There's Susan. Thank heaven, Prescott thought. She was alone no handlers to be seen. No Colonel Smith either. The force was with him, Prescott thought, the force was with him. Now is the time to strike.

"Frank is a Good Boy," Prescott said casually to Susan.

Susan stopped what she was doing, walked over to one of the chairs and retrieved the large binder with the translation documents and her own gravity propulsion notes.

Susan gave them to Prescott without a word. He grabbed them and darted down the corridor to the bedrooms. Prescott ran into the first bedroom, lifted up the mattress on the top bunk and pushed the binder with the translation documents and the gravity propulsion notes underneath the mattress as far as he could.

Prescott closed his eyes again. This time he had worked up a sweat and was breathing hard.

Calm down, he thought to himself, calm down. Mission accomplished.

Prescott peeked around the corner from the bedroom that lead to the open area where the dining room and restrooms were. No one in sight. He slowly eased himself out, and, seeing nobody was around, started walking confidently down the corridor.

Suddenly, through the open two-way window of the ship, Prescott saw Colonel Smith striding toward the saucer.

Prescott began to panic. He was unaccompanied without a handler. Susan was unaccompanied too. This could spell trouble for Bob and Jim, the handlers, who Prescott had come to know and like over the last three months. What to do?

Prescott saw Colonel Smith enter the saucer probably going to the bridge to see Susan. Prescott did a count down. One, two, three, go! Prescott scampered down the corridor as stealthily and quickly as he could and exited the saucer slowing up his gait and catching his breath.

Prescott decided to return to the canteen for lunch. As Prescott queued in line Priscilla and Roger her handler walked in. Then Bob and Jim walked in too. Prescott glanced at Priscilla wanting to blink her that he had the translation and gravity propulsion documents and notes.

Prescott found an open table and began eating his hamburger. Prescott knew Priscilla would probably either come over to his table, or if she didn't, he would.

Priscilla got her soup and salad and walked over to Prescott. Roger trailed behind her and sat down with them. It was a rule that work collogues didn't lunch together in the canteen even when accompanied with a handler. Over time that rule had been softened unofficially.

Bob and Jim sat down at a table not far from them. As far as Prescott could see they appeared nonthreatening in their deportment.

As Prescott took a large bite of his burger and as Priscilla took a bite of her salad Prescott blinked out, *Have docs.*

Priscilla, visibly nervous to Prescott, blinked back, *Ten Four.*

He was thinking he must be visibly nervous to her.

Colonel Smith walked up from out of nowhere.

"Frank (*Prescott*) and Sandra (*Priscilla*) hope you are doing well. Ready for the big day tomorrow?"

"Yes sir!" Prescott and Priscilla said together in the military style Colonel Smith liked.

"Great! Meet me in my office at 1600 hours. I need to go over some final details about the mission."

"Yes sir!" Prescott and Priscilla said together again even louder.

Colonel Smith grinned and walked away.

"They're great people," he thought to himself casting aside the doubts he'd been having about Frank (*Prescott*). "Everything's going to be fine."

After lunch Prescott and Priscilla were gratified to see the saucer being loaded with the supplies they'd arranged to have purchased or requisitioned for their flight to Zeta 2 Reticuli.

Colonel Smith was finishing up his chat with Prescott and Priscilla in his office.

"That's about it. If any one of you should be killed in the test flight, the insurance policies you signed will be initiated and your beneficiaries will be contacted and paid. It's an unpleasant topic to discuss, but necessary. Do you have any questions?"

"No sir," Prescott and Priscilla said.

Colonel Smith eyeballed them with affection.

"I wish you both the best of luck tomorrow. You've trained. You know the spacecraft as well as anyone. You know the mission. You're ready."

Bob the handler stepped in.

"Are you ready?" he asked.

"We're ready!" Prescott and Priscilla responded.

Prescott surmised a dog and pony show for the benefit of Section Chief Colonel Smith and the two handlers Bob and Jim was in order.

"Ready! Ready! Ready!" Prescott began chanting.

Priscilla quickly joined in until all five of them were shouting in unison, "Ready! Ready! Ready!" for two minutes.

Colonel Smith got up from his desk and hugged Priscilla, then Prescott.

"Tomorrow at 1100 hours you launch," Colonel Smith said. "Go catch the bus now. Go home and get a good night's sleep."

"Godspeed," he said, beginning to exhibit emotion, knowing the mission was not without its dangers.

Bob and Jim were silently thinking to themselves they'd probably overanalyzed and had been paranoid in their assessment that Frank (*Prescott*) had hypnotized Susan.

The kid was simply a smooth operator.

As Prescott and Priscilla were flying back from Area 51 to McCarran International Airport in Las Vegas they were concentrating on the next part of their plan.

They had both suppressed any moral qualms about what they were doing and were focused on executing the practical aspects of the plan now.

As soon as they got to their government issued cars, they disabled GPS tracking. Priscilla had piggybacked her knowledge of scrambling calls on iPhones and applied it to the GPS tracking on their cars.

They both hit the I-15 northbound heading for Area 51. They knew the route like the back of their hand and all the roads they needed to take. Their cars were in excellent mechanical shape and full of gas.

They turned left from I-15 onto U.S. Route 93, then left from U.S. Route 93 onto Nevada State Route 375 westbound also known as the Extraterrestrial Highway.

Prescott and Priscilla had made careful time studies and decided a five-minute increment between their arrivals at Area 51 would work and would be the most plausible to the gate guards.

At the first guard gate they encountered after exiting Nevada 375 they presented their documents and conveyed their well-rehearsed rational for making entrance onto the base after hours.

As expected, they were waved through.

At the second guard gate they were waved through without incident.

The tricky part was the drive to Sector 4 because the last third of the drive was on a rough-hewed road. Their cars were in top shape and it was a one-way trip.

As planned, they both parked their cars at the base of the mountain and walked to where they knew Hangar 7 was inside the mountain.

Two security guards with weapons approached them.

They explained another well-rehearsed set of falsehoods showing the guards their ID badges.

When one of the guards was about to balk, Priscilla's thinking on her feet came to the rescue, telling the guard their story could be confirmed inside the hangar. Prescott added that Colonel Smith would hate to be bothered at home about something that was nothing.

The one hesitant guard was won over cautioning them that their story could be confirmed inside the guard station in Hangar 7.

The guards opened Hangar 7.

The two-armed guards then escorted Prescott and Priscilla to the guard station inside.

It was 2124 hours and dark and cold. The sky was full of stars.

As the two-armed guards stood by, the guard in the guard shack inside the station was checking the computer monitor.

"By George, you're right," the guard said to Priscilla, who was trying to modulate her breathing. "The saucer is scheduled to be rolled out at 2100 hours. You say this is a pre-flight test?"

"Yes sir," Prescott said politely, putting on his method acting hat. "We're running late. Colonel Smith didn't want a lot of hoopla tomorrow morning when we actually launch."

Prescott knew this was the weak link of the plan. If this bluff failed and the guard contacted Colonel Smith the jig could be up. He'd have to come up with a cover story and quick if the guard called Colonel Smith and the Colonel wanted to talk to him.

"You're just doing a pre-flight?" the guard asked.

"That's right," he replied. "As you can see it's noted in the official itinerary in the system for 2100 hours this evening."

"No doubt about it it's right there in the system the ship is scheduled for a roll out at 2100 hours tonight. Why do you need the ship to be rolled out?" the guard asked, still not fully convinced.

"We need to be sure the aired waves are acceptable for the thrusters. I can only monitor that with the saucer out in the open air. That's the final part of the pre-flight. Colonel Smith didn't want to make a big deal about it tomorrow with all the activity that will be going on. He wanted to keep it hush hush for security reasons.

The night will be cold, but that will have no effect on the saucer. No inclement weather is in the forecast. Overhead enemy satellites won't be able to photograph the exposed saucer because we have a new invisible shielding system you don't know about. Top secret. You're not to say anything about it."

Prescott had calculated the bolder and more outrageous the lies, the more believable they would be to the guards, who were not versed in physics.

"Let me see your ID badges again," the guard said to them.

The Hangar 7 guard signaled to the two-armed guards they could return to their sentry duty outside.

The guard scanned the bar codes on their ID badges and passed the scanner over their eyes and right hands. Then they walked through the security tunnel.

"Is that luggage?" the guard asked about the four large pieces of luggage they had with them.

"No," Priscilla replied, "they contain some monitoring equipment we need for the aired waves test. It'll show up on the screening monitor. We'll just leave them out here if that is ok."

The guard didn't say anything, then he had a question.

"You need the hangar door to remain open?" the guard asked.

"Yes," Prescott said. "We need a roll-out team to get the saucer outside. I've seen it done a few times. I believe the prime movers are over there," he said, pointing to two large custom-made pieces of towing equipment staged alongside the wall.

"I've seen it done too," the guard said. "I think we have people on duty tonight who can do it. I've seen forklift drivers do it. The forklift drivers are all trained on the prime movers."

The guard made a call, then two muscular men approached the guard shack. The guard spoke with them, then they walked over to one of the prime movers and one of them got inside the cab while the other one guided. They rolled the prime mover down the short distance to the Executive Model saucer.

They attached clamps on the front struts and middle of the saucer in a process that had been designed decades ago to move the saucers around without damage. Usually it was the prime overs that got damaged, not the saucers.

"Alright Charlie, move it out!" one prime mover driver said to the other.

The saucer began to roll toward the open hangar door as the prime mover pulled it.

Soon the saucer was sitting on the desert ground forty feet from the hangar door opening.

"This far enough?" the driver called out to Prescott and Priscilla.

"Pull it out another twenty feet," Prescott cried out to the prime mover driver.

"Far enough?" the prime mover driver hollered.

"You're good. Thanks," Prescott hollered back as the driver began unhooking the prime mover from the saucer to return it to the hangar.

Prescott and Priscilla approached the guard.

"We're going inside the saucer to set up the monitoring equipment we need," Priscilla said to the guard.

The guard said, "You two are the ones who are going to take that saucer to the moon tomorrow, aren't you?"

Priscilla smiled at him as gracefully as she could. "That's right."

Priscilla pointed her iPhone at the saucer using the radio frequency she'd recorded from Colonel Smith's alien remote and opened the hatch door as the ramp extended and came to a thud on the ground.

They grabbed their suitcases and took them inside the saucer.

The ramp extracted itself from the ground and repositioned itself in the saucer as the hatch door silently closed shut.

Colonel Smith was dozing in his easy chair when his phone rang.

"Smith," Colonel Smith said.

"Good evening, Colonel. It's Roger. I'm sorry to disturb you at home, and I should have told you while I was at work, but there's something on my mind I need to share with you."

"What's that?" Colonel Smith asked, concerned.

"When I was in the lab today –," Roger began before Colonel Smith cut him off.

"Hold on Roger, I've got an incoming call. Let me put you on hold. Standby."

"Yes sir," Roger said.

Colonel Smith placed Roger on hold.

"Smith," he said once again.

"Colonel Smith, it's Susan Jones."

He got up from his chair.

"What's wrong Susan?" Colonel Smith asked.

"I don't know. I just don't know. I can't understand it."

"Understand what? Where are you?"

"I'm on Highway 93 at a convenience stop near Kingman, Arizona."

"Why are you there?"

"I don't know. I feel so disoriented. When I got home, I felt this compelling need to drive to Roswell, New Mexico. I have no idea why. I had to use the restroom and suddenly I asked myself why am I doing this? I don't feel well."

"Did you drive your government issued car?"

"Yes."

"Stay where you are. We'll track it."

"One more thing Colonel Smith. I think I gave the translation documents and my personal notes on gravity propulsion to Frank (*Prescott*)."

"Stay where you are!" he shouted to Susan. "That's an order!"

Colonel Smith had an epiphany. "Frank (*Prescott*) and Sandra (*Priscilla*)!"

Prescott and Priscilla quickly got the saucer ready to launch. According to Prescott's statistical calculations the probability was ninety percent that they were either being detected, or had been detected, by now. They had already defied the odds.

Prescott and Priscilla knew they had five minutes at best to lift off before security was alerted. After five minutes they would be destroyed if they got airborne.

"Ready on the thrusters?" Prescott cried out to Priscilla.

"Ready!" Priscilla confirmed

"Engage!" Prescott said.

The glowing saucer began to lift upwards wobbling a little.

Upon seeing the saucer moving the guard pushed a red button.

Loud speakers began blaring. SECURITY ALERT! SECURITY ALERT!

Colonel Smith just got his call in to the guard shack as the guard was calling him.

"Have you been visited tonight?"

"Sir, those two who are scheduled to take the saucer on the test flight tomorrow are taking off in it now. I've pushed the red button and alerted the air base."

"Shoot to kill!" Colonel Smith screamed out through tears as he saw his whole world crumbling before his eyes.

"Yes sir," the guard said. The security guard knew his job was finished. He'd never make retirement now.

The guard ran to the armed guards.

"Shoot it!" he screamed as the two-armed guards began unloading rounds that bounced harmlessly off the saucer as it steadied itself hovering fifteen feet off the ground.

"Picking up two aircraft moving toward us at high speed," Priscilla yelled out.

"That would be jets from the air base scrambled to shoot us down," Prescott said.

"Course set. Ready for second thruster control," she said, on her knees at the helm and navigation panels.

"Engage!" he said.

The saucer ascended at a rapid speed wobbling slightly as the two jets sent to intercept the saucer were rapidly approaching.

"Tracking two gremlins," Priscilla cried out frantically.

"I don't want to shoot them down," Prescott yelled out. "Go to third thruster until we're out of the atmosphere."

"Incoming!" she screamed seeing four heat-seeking missiles closing in on them fast.

"Evasive!" he shrieked, as the saucer shook and moved sideways and then upward avoiding the four missiles by 700 yards.

"Take us out!" Prescott yelled at the top of his lungs as Priscilla engaged full thrusters.

The saucer quickly left the upper atmosphere and was hovering over the Earth.

"Set course on impulse until we're out of the solar system," Prescott said.

"Aye, aye Captain," Priscilla said as she set the course.

They were on their way to the fourth planet called Serpo circling the binary star Zeta 2 Reticuli.

Colonel Smith considered suicide, but decided against it.

Colonel Smith, Susan, the three handlers Bob, Jim and Roger, the security guard and the two prime mover drivers were all placed under arrest.

"We can initiate Warp 1 in ten minutes, then I estimate we can get to Warp 6 in two hours and keep it there for the rest of our journey. We made it honey!" Prescott said to Priscilla.

"I can't believe we did it!" she squealed, beside herself with joy.

"To think of all that could have gone wrong," he pondered, awed they'd pulled it off.

"I thought for sure the radar locks from the jets would bring down the saucer like what happened in 1948," Priscilla added still shaking a little.

"I almost came to you this morning to abort this mission," Priscilla confided.

"I was thinking aborting the mission too this morning," Prescott said. "I'll never underestimate the power of luck again."

Priscilla opened her suitcase.

"Remember I told you about that Canadian band called Klaatu who named themselves after the alien in the sci-fi movie The Day the Earth Stood Still?" Priscilla asked.

"I remember you told me that band sounds like The Beatles in a way."

"I brought CDs with me. Listen to this song of theirs. It's called 'We're Off You Know'."

Priscilla pushed the play button of her CD player.

We're off you know to a distant land
And the only ones allowed to come are those who feel they can
Go right along with the master plan
And the only thing you've got to bring is sitting there in your head
(Is that all? That's all. That's all? That's all.)
So raise the sails and trim all the sheets
Set your course and jam all the cleats
We'll follow the north star to know where we are so
You sleepyheads get out of bed right now
Let your fortunes be cast to the wind
And so it's off we go to some uncharted shore
'Cause the only kind we're out to find are those worth looking for
You can tag along should you feel the urge to merge
'Cause we're all agreed that all we need is Hope and a little courage
(Is that all? That's all. Ooh hoo hoo)
So raise the sails and trim all the sheets
Set your course and jam all the cleats
We'll follow the North Star to know where we are so
You sleepyheads get out of bed right now
Get out the lead full steam ahead smartly now
For the journey begins
The journey begins
Our journey begins come the sun
Well wouldn't you like to go too ...?
Hey there you sleepyheads
Wouldn't you like to go too ...?
Get get up come on get up get out bed
Wouldn't you like to go too ...?
I said come on come on get up get out bed
Wouldn't you like to go too ...?
Get get get get up you sleepy heads
Wouldn't you like to go too ...?
Hey there, hey there, you sleepy heads

Chapter 12

Warp Factor 6

"We just passed Neptune and are coming up on Pluto," Priscilla said to Prescott.

"When we pass Pluto, we'll engage Warp 1 once we are 50,000 kilometers away from it," he directed.

"Why 50,000 kilometers?" she wanted to know. "No reason," Prescott replied, grinning.

"That's not scientific," Priscilla grinned back at Prescott, who was scooting around on her knees at the helm and navigation stations.

"Why don't you try sitting in the chairs?" Prescott suggested.

Priscilla looked over at Prescott giving him a look.

"Easy for you to say sitting in the regular sized captain's chair next to the alien captain's chair with nothing to do but give orders. My knees don't quite fit underneath the workstations. The chairs won't work for that reason. It's easier for me to just work on my knees on the deck. Who made you captain anyway?"

"You did. You know you're superior at helm and navigation than I am," Prescott said, suppressing a desire to laugh.

Priscilla stood up in mock anger. "You had the highest score in the simulation flight exam at 94. I came in at 83."

"You threw the exam honey," Prescott said attempting to placate Priscilla. "Besides, I'm three inches taller than you. If your knees won't fit underneath helm and navigation, mine surely won't."

"Are you going to hypnotize me next and make me the permanent helmsperson and navigator?" Priscilla asked only half joking.

"I think we should share the responsibilities of captain, helm and navigation equally," she declared.

"Agreed," Prescott said. "Let's switch off on a daily basis," he said, thinking there was something important they needed to discuss. Then he remembered. "One of us must be on the bridge at all times."

"True," she acknowledged, with a qualifier.

"Autopilot would probably be safe and theoretically we would never have to be on the bridge. This ship flies itself. The most important thing we have to do is monitor the reactor containment field.

Susan told us during training the emergency display indicator is on both the helm and navigation panels and the first officer's workstation. Susan told us while she couldn't find validation in the translation documents a ship wide red alert probably sounds in the event there is a problem with the containment field.

Monitoring the containment field could be an argument for having a main engineering."

"If something bad did happen to the containment field while we're on our way to Serpo, I don't think there is much we could do to rectify the situation," Prescott cautioned.

She moved her head back and forth in agreement knowing if something did go wrong with the containment field they would probably be destroyed in short order. There was no sense in worrying about something they had no control over.

"Our biorhythms are set-up for a 24-hour cycle," Priscilla observed. "Let's follow what comes natural to our bodies. We'll go on 8-hour shifts you take one shift while I sleep and I'll take one shift while you sleep and we'll figure out the rest as we go along. Maybe we can share four hours together on the bridge. We'll improvise."

"Sounds like a pragmatic approach," he agreed, realizing there was something else they needed to discuss.

"What about our sleeping arrangements?" he asked hesitatingly.

"Now that you've brought that up," she replied, "I was thinking we each take a separate bedroom for now. I believe we need to think this through, if you know what I mean."

"I know what you mean," Prescott said. "I believe that's a good way to handle things for now. Right?" he said, looking for reassurance.

"Right," she said emphatically, exhibiting a sureness that really didn't reflect reality.

"That reminds me," he said, "I've got to get the translation documents and Susan's gravity propulsion notes from under a mattress."

Prescott walked into the first bedroom, lifted up the mattress on the top bunk and retrieved the binder with the translation documents and gravity propulsion notes and rejoined Priscilla on the bridge.

"Here they are. These documents could spell the difference between life and death during our voyage."

"Let me see them," she said excitedly. Priscilla began sifting through them then, remembering Pluto, she checked the helm readouts.

"We're way past 50,000 kilometers beyond Pluto. We can go to Warp 1 at any time."

Prescott steadied himself in his chair. "Warp Factor 1," he said with flare, smiling at Priscilla.

"Warp Factor 1 set," she said with equal flare.

"Engage!" Prescott called out grinning. He looked at his watch. "In twenty minutes, we can go to Warp 2, in another twenty minutes Warp 3 until we reach Warp 6."

Priscilla keyed in commands to helm control. "I've set the helm accordingly," she said. "We'll be at Warp 6 in two hours. You know what we should do?" Priscilla asked.

"What?" Prescott retorted.

"Take inventory of the food supplies. I've set the helm on autopilot. We can safely check our supplies. We've got to unpack and unbox and put our food and water supplies away."

"Yes, you're absolutely correct. I'm getting hungry."

Prescott got the two retractable knives he had in his suitcase and gave one to Priscilla. "We'll open the boxes with these," he said. "Excellent," she responded, pleased that he had brought something useful with him she'd overlooked.

"You're sure the auto-pilot is safe then?" Prescott asked.

"Should be."

"You can't give me complete certitude?"

Priscilla looked askance at Prescott.

"I can't give you complete certitude about anything having to do with the operations of this ship or our mission or our safety. You're the top pilot here why are you asking me?"

Prescott sighed without saying anything.

"Come on, let's open these boxes and start putting things on these shelve units," Priscilla said.

Prescott saw four large boxes labeled Cracker Snackers. "Wonderful!" he declared with glee.

"Put the knife safety on," Prescott cautioned. "I'd hate for us to cut ourselves out here."

"Done already, but thank you for thinking about my safety," Priscilla replied.

Prescott eagerly cut off the straps off the set of four large boxes of Cracker Snackers.

As Prescott was cutting the straps off, he realized he missed the smaller print delineating the type of Cracker Snackers that were resident within each box. "Easy Melt," Prescott said out loud. "Ok, I did ask you buy some of those," Prescott grumbled to himself.

Priscilla looked over at Prescott. "I didn't hear you honey. What did you say?"

Prescott noticed the second and third sets of boxes were also labeled Easy Melt.

"How many boxes of Easy Melt Cracker Snackers did you buy?" he asked annoyed.

"What are you talking about?" she said.

"Remember the night I told you about the comfort foods I wanted for the voyage? I told you to get seventy-five percent Crispy Cracker Snackers and twenty-five percent Easy Melt Cracker Snackers.

All four boxes in this pack are Easy Melts. What happened to that famous photographic memory of yours? I wanted the Tongue Scorcher Cracker Snackers to be fifty percent of the total."

"Jim and I split up the buying when we went to the wholesale food store. He was responsible for buying the Cracker Snackers. Don't you like the Easy Melts?"

"They stick to the roof of my mouth and get in between my teeth," Prescott said, checking out the last four-box group of Cracker Snackers.

"Then why didn't you ask they all be the Crispy kind?"

"Because occasionally I like the variety," he blurted back, relieved that one of the boxes was all Crispy Cracker Snackers and not wanting to have to explain himself.

"Well, I have one-fourth Crispy and three-fourth Easy Melt. Not an auspicious start to our inventory."

"I'll help you eat the Easy Melts," she volunteered.

Priscilla was suppressing a grin with a naughty look on her face.

"What's going on?" he demanded to know.

Priscilla walked over to a tall stack of bottled water and dragged another set of four boxes of bags of Cracker Snackers from behind the bottled water where she had hidden them.

"Surprise! You have four boxes of Tongue Scorcher Cracker Snackers bags!"

"Wonderful!" Prescott exclaimed, trotting over and starting to slash the strapping anxious to grab a bag of Tongue Scorcher Cracker Snackers.

Prescott took out a bag of Tongue Scorcher Cracker Snackers from one of the boxes noticing they were of the Easy Melt variety and not his favorite the Crispy variety. "I'll eat them later."

Prescott took the boxes of Cracker Snackers and stacked them next to the still empty shelving units.

"Let's see what else we've got."

After an hour they'd opened most of the boxes and had placed the various canned goods and soups and coffee and bottled water and such on the portable shelving units.

Another small crisis cropped up when Prescott realized no ginger ale had been purchased for the trip, which would make it difficult for him to eat the Tongue Scorcher Cracker Snackers. Priscilla agreed she would share the sparkling soda she'd originally bought for her exclusive use. Priscilla had also brought a large stash of cranberry juice on board too.

They calculated if they were conservative in their eating habits the temptation of junk food notwithstanding, they could stretch the food supply out to eleven weeks for a round trip.

Using the long dining room table as a staging ground Priscilla set out the two microwaves ovens, two small refrigerators, two toasters, a coffee maker and a water purifier.

She put two can openers and bowls, glasses, plates, forks, spoons and knifes on one of the shelves.

Prescott's phone pinged. "We should be at Warp 3 by now. Can you go check?"

"Will do," Priscilla said.

She saw that all was well on the empty bridge with the warp drive increments set on auto-pilot.

"On schedule at Warp 3," Priscilla said as she returned. Prescott set his phone to ping when Warp 6 was scheduled to initiate.

She was lost in thought observing the two 55-gallon trash barrels and 100 large plastic trash bags with twists placed along the wall.

"As we accumulate trash eventually those two trash barrels are going to be full. Where are we going to put our trash after the two barrels fill up?" she asked.

"Good question," he replied. "We should have bought more trash barrels. If we don't find a solution to the trash problem the ship will begin looking and smelling like a city dump."

"I'm going over the translations with a fine-tooth comb," she stated. "You and I both know the Greys had a way to dispose of trash. We know about where the dumpster is, we need to figure out how to access it."

"What if they didn't create trash?" Prescott asked.

"They are so much like humans in other ways having restrooms and beds I have to believe they generated trash just like we do," Priscilla replied. "Entropy applies to them too."

"Maybe they don't have, or no longer have, a disposable society like we do," he countered.

"Maybe," she said not persuaded. "I'm going to have a look at those translations."

His phone pinged while he was making preparations for their first hot meal in space.

"I'll check to see if we are at Warp 6 now," Prescott said to Priscilla, who was sitting at the dining room table intently reading the translation documents.

Prescott saw all was well on the bridge the ship was on course for Zeta 2 Reticuli at Warp 6.

"Warp 6 has engaged," he said walking back into the dining room area.

"Earth to Pris, come in. Did you hear me?" he asked seeing she was oblivious to everything except what she was reading in the translation documents.

"What?" Priscilla said, finally looking up.

"We're at Warp 6. Why don't you take a break? I'm about ready to heat up some chili. Is chili good for you? Would you like something else?"

"Yeah, give me tomato soup. No, make that ravioli. Ravioli and chicken noodle soup."

Prescott removed a can of chili, ravioli and chicken soup from the food storage shelves. He also opened a bag of Tongue Scorcher Easy Melt Cracker Snackers and poured a heaping amount into a large bowl resealing the bag with a large clamp.

"What do you want to drink?" he asked. "Our options are limited," he added, reminding her she'd forgotten to buy ginger ale for the journey. "You can have either sparking soda, bottled water or cranberry juice."

"I'll take a can of sparking soda please," she answered.

He set out the plates, bowls, glasses and silverware. She opened her warm sparking soda and poured it still intently reading the translation documents.

"Can you put some cans of sparkling soda in the refrigerator?" Priscilla requested.

Prescott placed six cans of sparkling soda into the small refrigerator placed at the end of the dining room table.

He popped open a can of chili, poured it into a bowl and placed it in the microwave setting the heating time for four minutes.

Prescott pressed the start button stunned how it worked without electricity.

"It's free energy the kind Nikola Tesla predicted that Colonel Smith mentioned in the briefing," Prescott speculated. "The free energy field or vacuum field somehow senses the required current and wattage from the microwave and supplies that amount. The microwave must draw the amount of power it needs no more no less."

"I got it! I got it!" Priscilla suddenly screamed out loud enough to pierce Prescott's ears.

"Got what?" Prescott asked with his mouth full.

"I found the instructions for activating the replicator, the laundry cleaner, meaning a washer and dryer all in one, which also doubles as a dishwasher as well as the trash disposal."

Prescott quickly swallowed. "Say what? For real? How?"

"Brains over brawn, Barr," she said teasingly as he smiled.

Priscilla walked over to where the replicator was supposed to be. After placing her hands in several places repeatedly a green outline appeared.

"There it is!" she said excitedly.

"Get another bowl of chili," Priscilla urgently directed Prescott. "Come on, get another bowl."

Prescott grabbed another can of chili from the pantry, opened it and poured it into another bowl.

She pulled back a handle built into the outline opening what looked like any oven anywhere.

Priscilla took the bowl of chili and put it inside and closed the door. She then keyed into a panel displaying the alien's numbering system.

"How long do you like your chili to cook?" She asked.

"I don't about this contraption, but I usually put mine on four minutes in a standard microwave," he replied.

Priscilla rushed back to the translation documents lying on the dining room table, then rushed back to the oven in the wall.

"If my bet is right, this should be right about four minutes," she said to herself as she keyed in some numbers.

The oven glowed a slight greenish hue while remaining silent. Prescott was keeping time. "Two minutes," he said. The glow continued. "Three minutes," he called out.

Then at three minutes and fifteen seconds the glowing stopped.

Priscilla took it out and quickly placed it on the table since the bowl was hot. Prescott took a spoon and tried it. "Good, just the temperature I like. Now we have our own built-in microwave oven."

"Oh yeah?" she said smugly.

Priscilla walked over to the microwave oven, or wall oven, or food replicator or whatever it was. "Look at that!" she exclaimed in awe.

Prescott rushed over.

What looked like a photo of the bowl and chili inside it was superimposed over what appeared to be an icon that had suddenly appeared just below the oven.

"What does it mean?" Prescott asked.

"It means our food problems are over," Priscilla replied as she pushed the icon.

The oven glowed again and exactly three minutes and fifteen seconds it stopped. Priscilla opened it and an exact duplicate of the bowl full of warm chili was sitting there.

Prescott's mouth was wide open and not because he was hungry.

Priscilla slowly reached in and removed the bowl of chili and sat it on the dining room table. "Try it," she told Prescott.

He tentatively took a spoon full. "Not bad, although it is a bit bland," he commented. "But not bad. It'd work on a desert island."

Priscilla began waxing scientific.

"In some unbelievable way the molecular makeup of the chili and the bowl must be recorded and transitioned using an unknown source of matter. Or, it must do regenerative recycling from the ship's trash and – well, you know. I'm sure it's purified. When you heated up your chili it remembered the pattern and replicated it."

"And gave us a cool icon," Prescott said reverently, "for future use. I know! I bet it can make me an unlimited supply of Tongue Scorcher Crispy Cracker Snackers! Talk about 3D manufacturing. Think of the jobs this technology could wipe out."

Prescott got a bag of the Tongue Scorcher Crispy Cracker Snackers, put them in a bowl and set them to heat up for approximately one minute as Priscilla set the time for him. When she shut the door, the oven glowed again.

After about forty seconds the glowing stopped. Prescott eagerly opened the oven door only to find the bowl was full of red powder. Prescott dipped his index finger into the bowl and took a taste. "Terrible!" he exclaimed in disgust, quickly putting the bowl down on the table.

An icon with the bowl and red powder suddenly appeared next to the icon with the bowl and chili.

Priscilla doubled over in laughter and had to sit down to catch her breath.

"I suppose even the aliens aren't perfect," Priscilla managed to say between outbursts of mirth. "The molecular structure of your Tongue Scorcher Crispy Cracker Snackers must be too complicated for their replicator to reproduce."

Priscilla kept trying not to laugh as Prescott glumly stared at the bowl of red powder.

Prescott continued eating his chili as Priscilla dived into her ravioli and chicken soup.

Prescott looked at his iPhone.

"My emails, texts and incoming and outgoing calls are all blank and gone," he said in semi-surprise. "So are my apps and some other buttons."

"What did you expect? We no longer have internet connectivity and no more cell towers. Our phones no longer serve a function except as a watch and we can still reference our photos."

"Let me try FaceTime."

"Waste of time," she chided shaking her head, wondering why he would bother.

"Nothing," he conceded after trying to connect with Priscilla's FaceTime function on her iPhone.

Prescott was eating Tongue Scorcher Crispy Cracker Snackers from a bowl getting his fingers red as he slurped on sparking water soda in between bites.

"Did you hear me ask my question?" Priscila asked after swallowing some ravioli. "What would be the time and date if we were still in Las Vegas?"

"Sorry; yes, I heard you. Let me check the clock on my phone. The crystal oscillator inside our iPhones should still be sending out electrical signals. Ok, my clock says it's 2:36 AM. I noted we left the Earth's atmosphere at 8:34 PM on Wednesday November 21st. It's now 2:36 AM, or 0236 hours as Colonel Smith would say, on Thursday morning. We've been in flight for six hours."

Prescott pushed his bowl of Tongue Scorcher Easy Melt Cracker Snackers away, grabbled a roll of paper towels and began wiping the red off of his fingers. He'd have to do a test run of the faucet in the restroom because the red wasn't coming all off.

Prescott knew he'd have to brush his teeth as he struggled to dig gooey snackers out from in between his teeth and the roof of his mouth caused by the fact the snackers were of the Easy Melt variety. He wished all of his Tongue Scorcher Cracker Snackers were of the Crispy variety.

Prescott asked himself it he'd brought enough toothpaste. Cracker Snackers require a lot of toothpaste.

Priscilla looked at Prescott. "Well, it was bound to happen. I've got to go to the bathroom."

"I put a roll of toilet paper next to each toilet," he called out after her.

Five minutes later she returned.

"How did it go?" he asked.

"As well as could be expected. It's set on a rotating sequence. Remember when Colonel Smith mentioned the bidet analogy during his briefing? It has a self-cleaning system and toilet paper isn't needed. The auto flush feature worked perfectly. It flushes when the sensor detects movement away from the toilet."

"Describe the self-cleaning system."

"Everything is done using a quick sequence of wetting and drying."

"But how does it know when you're finished?"

"Take my word it works honey."

She didn't wish to delve any further into the nitty gritty details.

"I'm going to find out about this rotating sequence in person because I got to go myself."

Priscilla found the trash receptacle in the floor of what they called the kitchen. There was a foot lever that was noticeable once you knew it was there. The trash magically disappeared. So much about the spaceship was like magic.

Prescott cited her discoveries as a reason why they needed the translation documents before leaving.

"You'll take the day shift then?" Priscilla asked.

"Yes. Might as well kick this off. Like we were saying we'll switch off eight-hour shifts. I'm tired, but somebody has to be on the bridge we can't leave it unattended for hours on end."

"Hypothetically we could," she countered. "The auto pilot works just fine. What if you split your eight-hour shift into two mini-shifts of three hours each giving you two hours to take a nap?"

Prescott considered Priscilla's proposal. They both hadn't slept in 20 hours and they had been incredibly stressful hours. They were both on high alert and punchy and running on empty.

"If you're as tired as me you'll go to bed right now and just sleep. You must be exhausted because I am," she remarked, wondering if they would really continue their pact of sleeping in separate bedrooms, even though the suggestion had been hers.

Prescott knew even if he was on the bridge, he would invariably fall asleep.

"Until we acclimate and our bodies are adjusted it is logical that we get the rest we need to maintain our health. Alright, the helm and navigation are already set at Warp 6. Let's go to bed," he said, a slight smile on his face.

"Which bedroom do you want?" she asked coyly.

"The first one. It's closer to the bridge," Prescott said, as he was contemplating their sleeping arrangements.

Because they were exhausted, they didn't spend too much time agonizing over their sleeping choices.

After making sure everything was set at the helm and navigation they retreated to their separate bedrooms.

Prescott and Priscilla immediately collapsed into bed as the saucer continued its journey to the fourth planet circling the binary star Zeta 2 Reticuli.

Prescott's alarm went off at noon. He reached over to the chair he's placed next to the lower bunk he was sleeping in and turned it off.

Due to the free energy available on the saucer Prescott and Priscilla had removed batteries from all of the extras they'd brought along including their portable alarm clocks and iPhones.

He'd slept like a log and still felt like he could use some more sleep as he suppressed a yawn. His thoughts turned to Priscilla wondering how her first night in her new bed had gone.

Prescott slowly sat up in bed and rubbed his eyes. He decided to follow the regimen he'd outlined for himself including shaving every day instead of growing a beard.

He got dressed. As he was exiting the bedroom with his razor and shaving cream in hand, he could smell freshly brewed coffee.

He walked into the dining area where Priscilla was taking some rolls out of the microwave.

"Good morning," she said. "I've got hot coffee and hot rolls. I have some jelly we can put on them but no butter.

"Good morning," Prescott said.

"That coffee smells good. How did you sleep?"

"I slept like a baby," Priscilla replied. "I got up 20 minutes ago. I had my alarm set for one o'clock, but woke up and decided to get going."

"Did you check the bridge?" Prescott asked. "Everything on course?"

"Yes. We're at Warp 6 and all is well. I also took a look at the reactor downstairs. It looks good purring like a kitten. I know, I can check it from the bridge, but I wanted to see it for myself."

"Good," Prescott mumbled as he wolfed down a roll with jelly and swigged his coffee.

"Wish we had milk. I have dry creamer. Let me get it," she said playing the role of host to repay Prescott for preparing her meal last night.

He was savoring the coffee. "That's good. Good antidote for jet lag."

"You mean saucer lag," she said as she sat down at the table.

Prescott felt the coffee beginning to wake him up.

"I'd better get going. I'm going to shave and try to find a way to take a cold sponge bath at the sinks. I also know they must have hot water. The Greys are like us in so many ways they must have used hot water too."

"I was thinking about all that myself," Priscilla said. "Logically they had hot water."

"Thank you for breakfast," he told her.

"You're welcome, sweetheart," she said.

Prescott nodded and walked toward the restroom area with his razor and shaving cream.

He'd seen the sinks work during his work on the saucer. Two sinks sitting just a little low were aligned along the wall across from the toilet and urinal and only cold water came out. Prescott chose the right sink and sat his can of shaving cream and razor down on an area seemingly designed for that purpose.

Did the aliens shave Prescott asked himself as he put his hand toward the back of the sink to the right as water cold dispersed although there was no obvious faucet. He withdrew his hand and it stopped. Then he put his to the left as hot water dispersed.

"Pris! Come here. I want to show you something. Priscilla! Where are you?"

"I'm coming," Priscilla cried back mildly alarmed thinking something bad had happened.

"I have hot water!" Prescott said in triumph. "If you place your hand on the right cold water comes out. If you place your hand on the left hot water comes out."

"Wonderful!" she said clapping her hands. He saw her eyes get large. "Look Prescott mirrors!"

Prescott whirled around on the balls of his feet. A small mirror was displayed in the wall over the right sink. Over the left sink a mirror was starting to come into view. With a little bending down he could see his face well enough to shave.

"The mirrors must be part of the power system on board. I wonder why it took so long for them to be displayed?" Prescott asked Priscilla.

"This saucer was dormant for decades," Priscilla speculated, looking at herself in the mirror. "Maybe the power systems for things such as the mirrors are just coming online. It seems embedded in the wall, but otherwise it's like any mirror on Earth."

"Amazing," Prescott exclaimed, "Like everything else on this ship. I'd better shave and get cleaned up. What are you going to do while I'm on bridge duty?"

"Get some more sleep. I'm feeling tired again. I bet you are too."

"I am," he acknowledged. "It'll take a few days for us to totally acclimate. Don't worry about me."

"Tell you what," she said. "I'll relieve you in six hours. How's that?"

"Sounds good," he replied. "I'm feeling tired again too."

"Get cleaned up and I'll go to my bedroom and go back to sleep," Priscilla said teasingly, emphasizing 'my bedroom'.

Prescott placed his hand to the left and hot water came out. He splashed hot water on his face until the water auto stopped after about thirty seconds. Then he bent over slightly and began shaving.

Prescott noticed Priscilla had placed clean towels on racks that were like any bathroom towel rack you'd find anywhere on Earth. That meant the Greys used towels.

He was about to leave the head as he was beginning to call the restroom using the nautical term when he decided to take a look at the one and only area that a shower could be if they had one. Prescott was sure they did despite the fact no word had been found in the Greys translation documents on shipboard operations.

The area was a corner where the flooring had a different appearance almost like tiles. On a lark Prescott went to the corner and stuck out his hands toward the wall. A stream of water not too hot and not too cold suddenly emitted. He quickly stepped back as some water splashed on him. The water ceased.

Prescott ran to Priscilla's bedroom.

"Pris, guess what!" Prescott said as she struggled to wake up.

"What?" she asked.

"We have a shower!"

"Really!" Priscilla said happily, waking up. "I'd like to see," she said.

"No, honey, stay in bed. Get your rest. I'll show you when you relieve me on shift. In the meantime, I'm taking a shower. I've really needed to take one since I had that pick-up game with Bob and Jim."

"Pick-up game?"

"Yeah, basketball. I'll tell you later. Look it, go back to sleep. Sorry I woke you up I was excited."

"I'm glad you did. It's nice to know we have a shower. Is the water hot?"

"It feels comfortably just right. My guess is the temperature can be adjusted to individual preference. Go back to sleep. We might find out eventually from the translations. See you later."

"See you later," Priscilla said as she lay her head back down on her pillow.

Prescott went next door to his bedroom and retrieved a change of underclothes. He then returned to the shower area. In the meantime, a partition had appeared. Prescott tentatively moved his right hand toward the partition that was not unlike a shower curtain in appearance and his hand went through it.

How is that possible? Simply unbelievable. Prescott reasoned the spacecraft itself was unbelievable so what else is new?

He walked through the partition and stuck out his hands toward the wall again and the water gushed forth from a shower faucet that had appeared out of nowhere.

Prescott undressed placing his clean underclothing on a second rack next to the first rack with the bath towel.

He eased into the shower. Ah, that feels good, he was thinking. Prescott looked down at his feet and saw that the water wasn't accumulating on the tile, but was instantly evaporating.

Prescott took a bar of soap and began rubbing it all over his body. Prescott experimented seeing if the water temperature was somehow linked to hand motions. The water temperature and water pressure remained fixed and was comfortable enough.

Better leave well enough alone, Prescott decided. The water was spurting out of the shower nozzle slightly below his eye level so for average sized Grey aliens the was several inches above them. It was movable and its angle could be adjusted.

He was remaining in the shower for an extended time. All of a sudden, the shower curtain partition disappeared along with the water stream. Looks like my shower is finished, Prescott thought, as he groped for the towel on the rack since he'd managed to get soap in his eyes and they were stinging.

He was asking himself why would the partition fade out at the same time the water flow stopped? Either that was a design flaw, or there was a way to reinstate the shower curtain for modesty.

Whatever, Prescott decided, as he managed to open his eyes just long enough to see the towel. Prescott stepped away from the shower area and began drying himself. There was no water on the floor it was completely dry.

Prescott's eyes were stinging badly from the soap. He heard a noise. What was that?

Suddenly he heard a squeal. "Oh!" It was Priscilla. What is she doing here?

Prescott retreated back toward the corner wanting to restart both the shower and more importantly the shower curtain, such as it was.

"Sorry," Prescott heard Pricilla say, "I have to go really bad."

Prescott decided then and there the alien's restroom design left a lot to be desired.

Their design flaw had allowed him to be viewed butt naked by his girlfriend before they had been intimate.

Their design flaw had allowed him to know about his girlfriend's urgent and unstoppable intestinal force than he cared to know.

Too much information.

Chapter 13

Baby It's Cold Outside

Two weeks had passed since they left Area 51. Prescott and Priscilla had avoided mentioning the restroom incident out of courtesy to each other.

They had settled into a routine. They had meshed with the rhythm of the ships 15-hour dim and light cycles and had developed a shift rotation process based not so much on hours but on how the other felt to minimize negative effects on their health. Despite that they were averaging six hours a shift each and had managed to budget in several hours a day to be together.

From reading the translations Priscilla located the individual lighting controls in each room that could override the 15-hour dim and bright lighting cycles.

Playing chess together was their favorite diversion, along with listening to mostly classical music on the CD player Priscilla had brought with her. They both tried to stay in shape by walking around the corridor several times a day at a brisk walk. The brisk walking helped to dissipate nervous energy.

Then they began having bad dreams.

Priscilla was on the bridge when she heard Prescott moaning. She hurried to his bedroom, where Prescott was sitting up in bed.

"What's wrong?" she asked with great concern.

"I had a bad dream. Worst dream I've ever had in my life. It was a nightmare. It was terrible. I dreamed you and me were in front of a firing squad. Colonel Smith was there. Bob and Jim and Susan were there too. We were begging for forgiveness."

Priscilla could see Prescott was upset.

"What does it mean?" she asked. "I had an unsettling dream a couple of days ago. It was similar. In my dream we were at Area 51 just before we stole the saucer, but decided to cancel the mission and we had the saucer rolled back inside the hangar. It wasn't a nightmare, more like a feeling of impending doom."

"Why didn't you tell me?"

"I figured it was a one-off thing. It's interesting our bad dreams had similar themes about leaving Area 51. You've got the master's degree in psychology. What do you think?"

Prescott eased himself back down on his bed.

"Freud believed dreams are an expression of repressed wishes that we would rather not admit to ourselves and are a sign of conflict within the psyche," he stated.

"Do you think it means we have regrets about what we've done?" Priscilla suddenly had a fit of weeping.

"I'm so sorry Colonel Smith," she cried as she sat down on his bed as he held her as she rocked back and forth in his arms.

Prescott's eyes started to tear up.

"We betrayed Colonel Smith and our coworkers. We betrayed our country and our MJ-12 security clearance," Prescott said joining Priscilla in her wailing.

"What were we thinking?" Priscilla said loudly. "We must have been crazy to steal the saucer. We've thrown our lives away. Why did we do it?"

Prescott turned Priscilla toward him.

"We discussed this before we left. We knew the consequences. We made a bad decision. Just because we're smart doesn't mean we can't make mistakes, even big mistakes, and stealing the saucer from Area 51 qualifies. We can't go back now."

"If we did return and turned ourselves in, we might get off with a reduced sentence, or reduced punishment."

"You really want to risk that? What we did is worthy of the death sentence. That's what we were told in our briefings when we joined Area 51. That is what we signed our names to stating under oath that we understood the ramifications and would accept the consequences of our actions."

"I know we can't go back," Priscilla said. "I know we would likely be executed, or at minimum face life in prison without parole. We had a long discussion weighing the pros and cons and decided to proceed. We knew it was wrong. I just didn't realize how wrong until now."

They held each other.

"All we can do is move forward," Prescott said.

"And live with our decision," Priscilla remarked, beginning to cry again, as did Prescott.

A week later Prescott was on the bridge when he heard Priscilla screaming. He bolted from the bridge and ran into her bedroom. Priscilla was sitting at her desk in her bath robe.

"Turn it off, turn it off!" she pleaded over the loud humming sound of her hair dryer.

Prescott frantically fumbled around and found the off switch.

Priscilla said in embarrassment, "For some reason, a brain freeze you could call it, I put batteries in the hairdryer and when I turned it on wham the double power of the batteries and free energy revved up the amps. I wonder if it still works."

Priscilla pushed the on button again and the hairdryer hummed in its normal fashion.

Her head was positioned at an uncomfortable 45-degree angle with half of the right side of her hair stuck inside the hairdryer.

"Try pulling my hair out slowly," Priscilla said.

Prescott dragged a chair over and sat down next to Priscilla. He gently tugged at her hair and could see it was rigidly encased inside the hairdryer. The distance between the hairdryer and the right side of Priscilla's face was only a few inches.

"My neck is hurting," she complained. "Let me lay on the bed. It might make it easier."

Prescott guided Priscilla over to her bed and she stretched out so Prescott could work on the hairdryer from his chair.

"Your hair is really stuck in there," Prescott said in frustration. "We may have to cut your hair."

"No, please let's try to get it out without doing that. I didn't bring a pair of scissors with me. Did you?"

"No. I didn't count on a hairdryer sucking your hair all the way in. I could use one of the kitchen knives."

"Please don't do that!" Priscilla exclaimed.

"I have an idea," Prescott said. "I brought my Swiss army knife with me. It has a small scissors. I'll be right back."

He went next door to his quarters and got his Swiss army knife. Sitting down he began to exam the situation like a skilled surgeon.

"Let's take a look at this hairdryer. No screws that I can see. That might make this difficult. I could use my flat knife and try to pop open the dryer. If I do that, it might break apart the plastic container and make it unusable."

"I'm hoping we can avoid that," Priscilla said. "Wait a second. What if we put the batteries back into hairdryer and this time have it set on outflow instead of intake? Maybe the doubled wattage power surge will cause enough force of air to blow my hair back out."

"Worth a try," Prescott said. "The only other options are to break open the hairdryer to get your stuck hair unstuck, or cut off some of your hair."

Prescott guided Priscilla back to her desk with her head tilted and her right hand holding on to the hair dryer.

Prescott put the batteries back into the hairdryer.

He made sure the hairdryer buttons were set on air outflow and off.

"Ready?" Prescott asked Priscilla. She meekly shook her head affirmatively.

"Soon as you turn it on and it starts to blow turn it off as soon as your hair is out. Let me place your right index finger on the off button. The high button is one click above the off setting.

When I say go push the button up one increment to high. You should probably turn it back off pretty fast. As you know the off button is between the high button at the top and the low button at the bottom. The dryer will push backwards so be aware of that. I'll be right here. Remember, when your hair is free push down one click to turn it off."

Prescott yelled out, "Go!"

She dutifully pushed the hairdryer to on as it made a loud whirring noise like an aircraft taking off and began throwing Priscilla's hair out.

"Ow! Ow!" Priscilla kept saying as she struggled to keep the hairdryer from slipping away from her hand as Prescott put his hand behind hers to make sure the hairdryer didn't fly out of her hand.

"Turn it off!" Prescott yelled out to Priscilla as he simultaneously pulled the batteries out of the hairdryer.

Priscilla turned off the hairdryer.

"Most of my hair is out," she said, noticing one group of strands hanging out of the hairdryer that had been torn from her head.

"Thank you, Pres. I only brought one hairdryer with me."

"Glad to help. I'm taking your batteries away."

"Good idea."

As Prescott removed the batteries from Priscilla's hairdryer, he noticed her bath robe was a shade too small for her size even though she was five foot two. Her undersized bath robe didn't leave much to the imagination.

When Prescott returned to the bridge, he kept thinking about it.

Maybe they needed to discuss and revisit the merits of their vow of celibacy.

It was still two weeks to Zeta 2.

The next day Priscilla woke up with a thought. She and Prescott needed to discuss the prospect of landing on the Grey's home planet. What then? Would they be allowed to return to Earth if they wanted to? Would the Greys allow them to return to Earth in one of their ships?

There were many possible scenarios and Priscilla knew she and Prescott hadn't fully discussed them. In fact, they'd been avoiding discussing this topic at all.

Priscilla suspected they had been numbed first by the success of their 'grand theft saucer' escapade and second by the realization of their moral culpability. Priscilla decided she didn't need to have a master's degree in psychology like Prescott to arrive at this conclusion.

The right side of her head was sore from all the hair pulling yesterday and she dabbed some antibiotic cream on some places along the right side of her head.

Priscilla had been studying the smuggled translation documents and had made another discovery. Now she knew how to enable the laundry unit in her bedroom consisting of a washer dryer dishwasher combo.

Priscilla walked over to where the laundry unit was supposed to be. After placing her hands in several places repeatedly a green outline appeared.

"Pres! Come in here!" She called out.

Prescott stumbled in as she was tooling around with a panel that looked exactly like the one used for the food replicator.

A small handle came into view. Prescott pulled it opening a lid and exposing a hole in the wall of what looked like a standard washer or dryer. A set of alien Grey writing was displaying on a panel next to it.

Prescott had a thought. "Maybe you can enable and bring one online in my bedroom too!"

They darted to his bedroom.

Priscilla repeated the process and after placing her hands in several places repeatedly a green outline appeared in the wall of Prescott's bedroom.

"Yes! I've got a washer too! If that's what it is."

"It's the laundry unit. What else could it be," she said. "I recognize some of the script. I think it says washing and drying instructions. I think they have their washers and dryers combined into one unit. This is fantastic listen to this. I'm pretty sure this can also be a dishwasher. No more dirty laundry. No more washing and drying dirty dishes."

Prescott extended his hand along the inside of the cylinder. "If we make it to Serpo I'm asking them how that's done."

She walked over to him forgetting that she was in her less than adequate bath robe and hugged him from behind.

He turned around and kissed Priscilla.

"I'm not ready to sleep," Prescott said as he kissed her more forcefully. "I'm ready to go to bed, but I'm not ready to sleep."

They continued to kiss. Prescott had been planning to talk to Priscilla about the possibility of amorous activity despite their hesitations.

Priscilla suddenly remembered something.

"Prescott," she said, "I forgot to bring birth control."

"You did," Prescott murmured, kissing her again. "So did I," he remarked.

"Seriously," Priscilla said, stepping away. "I completely forgot."

"We could use the rhythm method," he said, his ardor only increasing with her protests.

"What do you know about the rhythm method," she said, almost breaking into a giggle.

"I've read it's a way to have birth control without the pill or whatever it is. Have you had your period?"

"Actually, I should be fertile for the next few days. I don't believe an unwanted pregnancy would be to our advantage at this point in time. If ever there was a time for us to be logical it's now."

Priscilla shifted her bath robe closer to her body as Prescott returned to the washer.

"I need to do a load of laundry soon," he said. "Tell you what. Why don't you make us breakfast, or dinner, whichever meal it is now I'm losing track, and I'll get my laundry started."

"But you haven't studied the writing. We should read the instructions first."

"We should," he agreed. "But the Greys are basically like us. You know the Greys do a lot by auto control and sensors. My guess is you put your dirty clothes inside the washer dryer combo if that's what it is and it does an auto start. It probably cycles based on the amount or weight of the load to be washed and dried."

"Why don't you go to bed. You just got off your shift."

"I will as soon as I do my laundry. I'm also hungry. I need to eat something. You wouldn't want me walking around with dirty underwear, would you?"

"No, I wouldn't," Priscilla agreed, laughing. "Ok, do your laundry and I'll make us dinner. That's the meal on deck."

"Sounds like a splendid idea Doctor Waterford," Prescott said to Priscilla. "I'm glad you concur Doctor Barr," Priscilla said back to Prescott.

Priscilla went to the kitchen as they called the dining area while Prescott retrieved his dirty clothes from a trash bag that had been substituting for a laundry hamper.

Prescott shoved his dirty clothes into the washer dryer and shut the door.

"Come on, start," he said under his breath.

Sure enough, it started rolling. Prescott let out a whoop Priscilla heard from the kitchen.

Prescott forgot the laundry detergent. Prescott scooted to the kitchen and opened a laundry detergent bag with detergent tablets as he startled Priscilla.

"I got it working baby!" Prescott said to Priscilla heading back to his bedroom with two laundry detergent tablets.

"Great! Dinner will be ready in five minutes," Priscilla called out to him as he ran by her.

Prescott opened the door and as he expected the washer stopped as he placed the two tablets inside and shut the door and the washer restarted.

Fantastic, Prescott thought to himself as he walked to the kitchen.

"What's for dinner?" Prescott asked as he sat down.

"Beef stew and asparagus," Priscilla replied as she placed the dish of food in front of Prescott.

"Thank you," Prescott said, gazing at Priscilla with fondness. Prescott was thinking he could get used to this domestic bliss. It would be over in two weeks, unless they could settle on Serpo if the Greys would allow it.

Returning to Earth was looking less and less desirable by the day.

"This is good," he said.

"I think it's good because you're hungry."

"Could be," Prescott said as he finished up. "I still say you're a good cook."

"Thank you, baby," she said. "You're welcome baby," he said, enjoying their newfound use of the endearment baby.

Whoa!" Priscilla yelled out.

"What?" Prescott said in alarm.

Prescott looked down at the floor. Soapy water was oozing in.

"My laundry!" Prescott dashed for his bedroom.

The unit was still turning. Prescott quickly opened the door and to his surprise the clothes were hot from being dried.

"Well I'll be," he said as she came into his bedroom. "My clothes are dry. Almost dry. Let's see if the dryer continues spinning."

Prescott closed the lid and the dryer continued its spin cycle.

"Did you use detergent?"

"Yes. You saw me take a couple of those tablets from the detergent package. I wonder why it overflowed?"

"Look Prescott, the floor. The soapy water is evaporating. Like nothing happened. What a ship we're on!"

"True, but that doesn't explain why the water overflowed."

"My conjecture is their washers don't use soap and rejected the two laundry tablets. Which makes doing the laundry even easier."

Then the dryer stopped. Prescott reached in and grabbed a piece of underclothing and smelled it.

"Smells fresh and it's totally clean like brand new. The Greys sure know how to put together an efficient spaceship," Prescott marveled.

"Let's finish dinner," Priscilla suggested.

"Soon as I fold my laundry. Wouldn't want wrinkled shirts."

Priscilla and Prescott scheduled themselves for a serious rap session.

Before they got started Priscilla put in a CD of in her player, turned the volume to low so it would be soft and soothing background music and pushed the play button initiating Eine Kleine Nachtmusik.

"I love Mozart," Prescott complimented Priscilla.

"Thank you. That Mozart piece is uplifting. Soothing eclectic serenades and violin concertos from various classical composers will follow. To the business at hand. I think we need to cover these items. I made an agenda," Priscilla began. "I think we need to figure out what our goals are. I think we should first try to figure out what drove us to steal the saucer."

"Agreed," Prescott said. "I think we should discuss our future together."

"Agreed," Priscilla replied. Priscilla got the ball rolling.

"Why did we decide to steal the saucer? Remember that night when we were on the phone and I suggested it?"

"No," Prescott emphatically said. "We decided at the same time. Remember? You said something like 'Are you thinking?' and we laughed and then we blurted it out at the same time."

"I realize that Pres, but I was the one who didn't say anything to the handlers or Colonel Smith when I found out how to isolate and stabilize the Grey's equivalent to Element 115 for antimatter. I falsified the log. That was before we had our phone chat."

"I know, but remember how happy I was you didn't say anything? That makes me just as guilty. We were on the same wavelength. I didn't say, 'Oh, that's wrong you need to rectify it tomorrow', or something like that."

Priscilla thought about it. "I guess you are as guilty as I am."

"We're equally guilty," Prescott said to reassure Priscilla. "We both planned the snatch together. We both lied and cheated and betrayed everyone to do it."

"Why did we do it? You're the psychology person here. What's your take on that?"

"Because we're iconoclasts. Remember when we told each other we'd been diagnosed with autism when we were in our early teens? High functioning autism. Both of us. I knew when I saw you that day at the airport for the first time you were meant for me."

"I felt the same," Priscilla replied. "I love you Prescott."

"I love you too Priscilla. I think we're getting off topic, but's it's a pleasant diversion. I'll add we are both neurotic too. I think it's in our nature to be different that leads to something like our taking off with the saucer. But our nature is to be cautious too and obey the rules. It's a contradiction of sorts."

"But we still made a bad moral choice, didn't we?" she nervously asked.

"By society's standards we did. I'm not going to defend our actions. I admit they were wrong. You and me are otherwise model citizens never in trouble with the law and always being honest at least until we got to Area 51.

We were given the chance of a lifetime to work with alien technology and presented with a unique situation and opportunity. It triggered whatever it is within us that was latent to come to the surface that allowed us to steal the saucer."

Prescott let out a sigh.

Priscilla started to wax philosophical.

"We gave up an enormous income and the chance to eventually have solid success in our field of physics.

Have you studied religion and philosophy Prescott? I have. I was interested in atheism for a while. I read Das Kapital by Karl Marx. Translated from the German it means The Capital in the economic meaning of the word. Marx believed religion was the opium of the people that was designed by a capitalist society to keep the downtrodden down. What do you think?"

"I know about Marx though I haven't read his works. I recently changed from being agnostic to being religious in the sense I believe the universe is too ordered and the human body is too complicated for it to have arisen by random chance."

"You believe in God then?" Priscilla asked.

"I believe the universe didn't come about by random chance. If that means I believe in God then I do," Prescott replied with certitude and conviction.

"I believe in God too," she said.

"I've read the works of Spinoza a philosopher. Have you ever heard of him?" he asked.

She shook her head no.

"Spinoza believed that everything that exists is God but we can perceive only two of them thought and extension. He also believed God must also exist in dimensions beyond those of the visible world."

"Spinoza sounds like someone worth reading," she said. "I'm not sure if we've arrived at why we stabbed our friends in the back and stole the saucer, but I believe we've had a good start to the discussion.

If we can change the subject, what are our goals? We'll be arriving at Serpo in two more weeks.

By the way, have you thought about what happened to Colonel Smith and Bob and Jim and Susan and Roger? What about the others like the security guard on duty that night and the men who rolled out the saucer and who knows how many others? They must have gotten into trouble. I mean serious trouble."

Prescott noticed a tear beginning to roll down Priscilla's cheek even as he could feel a tear of his own forming.

He cleared his throat his voice breaking.

"They got into serious trouble no question. They probably were arrested and some of them may go to prison. Colonel Smith as the person in charge faced serious consequences.

Susan too because she knowingly went out on four dates with me and I assume she ended up driving to Roswell, New Mexico and she provided me with her gravity propulsion notes and the translation documents.

Bob and Jim messed up many times. Roger too. The way we fooled the security guards and the prime mover drivers. We were too clever by half. It's terrible what we did to them."

"What if one or more of them committed suicide because of us?" Priscilla cried out.

Priscilla and Prescott broke down sobbing holding each other for comfort as waves of remorse swept over them causing their discussion to come to an abrupt end.

They would discuss their goals at another rap session.

Chapter 14

Calling Occupants of Interplanetary Craft

One more week passed. They were a little more than one week away from Serpo. The closer they got to Serpo, the moniker they were now using full-time for the alien Grey's home planet, the more subdued and anxious they became.

Warp 6 was holding steady. They both had had some reservations about keeping the ship at a constant Warp 6 for the five weeks plus duration of the flight. Priscilla double-checked the antimatter fuel consumption and it was at the predicted rate.

They'd both lost several pounds making them even skinner than they were before. Neither of them had been eating much lately and they were still doing their brisk corridor walking burning up calories.

Prescott could tell he and Priscilla were becoming clinically depressed. This was a flashing red-light danger. That is why they'd been putting off the final part of their discussion where they had broken down into bitter tears that had ripped their guts out afterwards.

Priscilla was still looking for where the aliens kept their first aid supplies. It was a useful to have a mystery to solve. It kept her mind occupied.

They set aside time for a rap session to finalize their discussion from last week.

With a more week left before they reached Serpo they agreed they needed to have that talk.

It was Prescott's turn to make dinner. The meal schedule was getting monotonous. He set the replicator for baked beans and pears.

They ate in silence. Then Priscilla spoke up. "I didn't tell you. While I was on my shift, I found out how to engage a stall around the toilet. It's the same as the shower curtain at the shower. It's incomprehensible how matter can go through them yet you can't see through them."

Prescott finished chewing a mouthful of baked beans and had a question.

"How does it work? Is there a switch or something?"

"When you sit down on the toilet just bend over and wave your right hand an inch to the floor and voila there it is."

Prescott shook his head baffled.

"Now that's a question I'd like to ask the Greys. Why not just have a metal stall with a door around the toilet? What's up with that? Ditto for the shower. I imagine they have their reasons."

"Maybe it saves on weight. Cumulatively saving weight throughout the ship could help with energy conversation."

Prescott wasn't buying it.

"You know how light their metal is. Having partitions around the toilet and the urinal too wouldn't add much weight. Same goes with the shower stall."

Priscilla finished up her meal.

"Why don't you ask them when we get there? I think we're avoiding our discussion once again. Remember? Our goals? We scheduled a rap session for after dinner tonight."

Prescott knew she was right.

"Meet me on the bridge," Prescott said as he stood up. "We'll talk then."

"Be there as soon as I wash and dry the dishes."

Priscilla joined Prescott on the bridge during his shift. Priscilla gazed in rapture at the main viewscreen as the stars sailed by.

"Aren't the stars beautiful?" Priscila asked. Prescott was looking at Priscilla instead of the viewscreen.

"Beautiful," Prescott said as she pulled a chair over next to him.

"How far have we traveled now?" Priscilla asked, knowing Prescott was keeping tabs on that.

"According to the helm readouts during my last shift, using my conversion of the Grey's time frame reference, we've traveled 31.40 Earth light years," Prescott answered. "We still have 7.84 light years until we reach Serpo, or seven more 24-hour Earth days."

"You'll have to explain to me sometime how you were able to convert the Grey's time increments into ours."

"I will. I have to give Susan a lot of credit for that. I'm glad we haven't encountered any problems except the late appearance of some ship operations."

"Or disappearance," Priscilla said blurting out laughing.

"Oh, you mean when I was groping around nude with soap in my eyes and the shower curtain disappeared?"

She began guffawing until she had to gasp for air.

"I swear that was the funniest situation I've been in my whole life," Priscilla finally commented after calming down.

Prescott grinned at her.

"It was funny. I mean, it wasn't too funny at the time, but it's funny now. Time heals all wounds."

Priscilla turned serious. "I hope so. You want to discuss our goals now?"

"Yes. Why don't you get us started? What do you envision for our future?"

"I see us being a couple for life no matter where life leads us."

"Me too, honey," Prescott said leaning in toward Priscilla as she met him halfway and they kissed.

"Now that we're an item everything else will take care of itself."

"I agree. That kind of cuts this conversation short. We should discuss what we're going to do when we reach Serpo. Any thoughts?" he inquired.

"A few. What if the Greys aren't happy to see us? Knowing them they'll track us pretty quickly. They might be tracking us now. What if they shoot us down?"

"Then all of our problems are solved," Prescott said deadpan.

"It would be romantic you and I perishing together like two star-crossed lovers going down with the ship."

Prescott grinned broadly at Priscilla. "Well said. That would be like you and me going down on our own Titanic."

"We'd be playing the role of Isidor and Ida Straus. I love that movie."

"Hopefully the Greys will be friendly and not like a hidden iceberg in the North Atlantic. Which one of us is going to land the saucer?"

"I think you should Pres," Priscilla suggested. "I piloted the saucer when we took off. I think it's only right that you be the one who lands the ship."

"That would make you the Captain," Prescott said as he reached out and gave Priscilla a friendly shove on her arm.

"It would wouldn't it?" she said as she laughed.

"It's a deal then," he said as they shook hands.

"Back to the reception we can expect from the Greys," Priscilla said. "There are simply too many variables to try to formulate a response for each one. Let's just hope for the best."

"That's a logical way of looking at it. Not much we can do in any case. The Greys will do whatever they're going to do and not much we can do aside of doing our best to be friendly."

"We do have the photon torpedoes," she mentioned. "But we shouldn't try to defend ourselves if they object to our arrival. Like you said, if they shoot us down all of our problems are solved. We'll die together."

"I totally agree," he said. "We'll hope for the best."

Priscilla pointed to the helm and navigation panels.

"I found red residue traces of Tongue Scorcher Cracker Snackers on the conn. I didn't bring any cleaner with me. I cleaned it off with water and paper towels."

"Sorry about that," Prescott remarked. "The other night I got into a bag and wolfed them down including a couple cans of sparkling soda. I was checking the helm and that's how the residue got there. I promise to be more careful."

"Please do," Priscilla said in a mocking tone, then she burst out laughing. "I find it hard to get mad at you. Have we had our first fight yet?"

"I think we have. I put you through the ringer when I found out you'd bought too many of the easy melt snackers and not enough of the crispy types despite my precise and unequivocal instructions to you. Let's not forget the ginger ale you forgot either."

Prescott was moving his right index finger at Priscilla in dramatic fashion.

"You're not going to let me live that down, are you?" Priscilla said grinning.

"I forgive you," Prescott said as he stretched his neck and kissed Priscilla.

They held each other for a couple minutes knowing the depressed feelings they were having were lurking under the surface of their superficial outward appearance of happiness.

I'm going to get some sleep now," Priscilla said as she gave Prescott a peck on the cheek.

"Good night, sweetheart," Prescott called out after her as Priscilla smiled on her way to her bedroom and hopefully a good night's rest.

Prescott checked in on Priscilla who was already getting ready for the day shift.

"I've been thinking," Priscilla began. "We have unlimited food with the replicator. We need to eat more not less. We've lost too much weight. If we lose much more weight, we'll be able to sit comfortably in the alien's chairs on the bridge. I will. You still may not be able to because you're three inches taller than I am. But since you've lost so much weight you might be able to."

Prescott looked at Priscilla knowing she was covering her general negative moodiness with nervous conversation.

"I know we've been bummed out lately," he said, beginning a short sermon. "We've got to get a grip. We've got to surmount these psychological feelings. Yes, we stole a saucer. Yes, we violated our oath. Yes, we possibly put lives in jeopardy."

She cut him off while chewing.

"Not possibly, definitely."

"What are they going to do execute Colonel Smith? They won't do that," he offered in defense.

"That's not what I mean," she said testily. "What if he killed himself? You know how much pride the man had in the mission. In you and me."

Priscilla could feel the guilt swelling up inside her again.

"You're in a mood today," he said bluntly.

"I'm sorry. I apologize. It's my nerves. I had another bad dream."

Prescott reached his hand out to Priscilla's.

"I'm sorry you had a bad dream."

She steadied herself changing the subject.

"I've been thinking about our sustaining Warp 6. We've been at Warp 6 for over four weeks. How many days until we reach Serpo?"

"Seven days."

"I'm thinking for safety reasons we should throttle back to Warp 5 for the remainder of the trip," Priscilla cautioned. "It shouldn't add too much time to the trip, should it? You do basic math better in your head than I do. How much longer would it take us to reach Serpo is we go to Warp 5?"

"Six more days."

Priscilla decided to second guess herself.

"Six more days. We've come this far at Warp 6 why stop now? I'm ready to get off this magic carpet ride."

"That was a good thought Pris. But I'm with you. Let's stay the course at Warp 6."

As their rendezvous with Serpo got closer and closer Priscilla and Prescott were becoming restive and pensive tinged with excitement and anticipation.

They had a special rap session going over what they wanted to ask the alien delegation or whoever among the Greys would meet them. The old question of whether they would be treated as enemies or friends came up again and again.

Prescott and Priscilla decided any species advanced enough for interstellar flight wouldn't be unduly alarmed by aliens meaning themselves showing up. The Greys would be used to the reality.

Not to mention that according the briefing they'd received that first day at Area 51 the Greys had been monitoring and visiting Earth for centuries. They decided it was to their advantage to be traveling in one of the Grey's spacecraft.

One day before their arrival they went over landing procedure protocols. They underwent several training simulations under different conditions each one taking turns landing the saucer although it was agreed that Prescott would have the honors.

If the aliens contacted them, they would follow their directions. If the aliens didn't contact them, they'd do their best to land in a viable location and hope for the best. They reinforced the idea they needed to land in or near a populated area. They didn't need to land in the middle of the alien's equivalent of the Mojave Desert.

Prescott and Priscilla knew they were about to embark on something incredible and history making. They decided to do their best to keep a daily journal not knowing exactly what would be considered a day on Serpo. The iPad Priscilla had brought with her would serve that purpose.

Now they were three hours away.

The star Zeta 2 Reticuli was plainly in view through the viewscreen. It's sister star Zeta 1 Reticuli was also visible at a greater distance away, but it a good deal brighter than the other stars.

They couldn't sleep and shared the last shift on the bridge together making sure their ready kits were properly provisioned.

How the saucer could have been out of use for so many decades after having been damaged and perform flawlessly impressed Prescott and Priscilla and was a clue the Greys were a formidable species of humanoids.

Now they were one hour away.

"How you doing?" Priscilla asked.

"Good," Prescott replied. "I'm doing good, Captain," he laughed as she gave him a kiss on the cheek.

"If it's ever discovered back on Earth that we actually made contact with the Greys in person on their own planet, assuming they don't shoot us down or kill us on sight, we'll be in the history books forever," Priscilla thought out loud, waxing philosophical as she was prone to do.

"True enough," Prescott agreed. "This is bigger than the moon landing. This is," he stopped mid-sentence. "Nothing compares with it. Remember when Colonel Smith said to have something ready that will top, 'One small step for a man, one giant leap for mankind'?"

"I remember him saying that," she said. "How about Take us to your Leader."

"If you can put us up for the night, we'll be on our way in the morning," he said.

"We're lost and were wondering if you can give us directions," she added.

He threw in one more. "Klaatu barada nikto."

They managed to smile at each other's wisecracks knowing their lives would be unalterably changed for good or bad very soon.

Priscilla had put the alien chairs back at helm and navigation because due to her weight loss she could now snuggly sit in the chairs without hindrance.

They could now see the Grey's home planet Serpo circling Zeta 2 through the viewscreen.

"Pris," Prescott said, "Why don't you land the saucer? It's easier for you to sit there and work the control panels. I still have trouble getting in and out of those chairs even if they are the alien originals and even after having lost who knows how many pounds."

"You sure?"

"Sure. Besides, I'll be the Captain again."

"Pulling rank on me, are you?" she said as they embraced.

"Are you scared?" he asked.

"A little bit. I have some apprehension. I think we need to stay on our toes now. How much longer until we reach their upper atmosphere?"

"Forty minutes," Prescott said. "I could be off by five or ten minutes one way or the other, but that's a reliable ETA. Priscilla, if we don't make it, if they send a hostile greeting party to meet us, I want you to know I love you. I love you because you're my best buddy."

"Thank you, Prescott," Priscilla said. "You're my best buddy and my best friend. I love you more than you know. We still have time to be intimate."

"I wanted to," Prescott said, remembering that night when they almost succumbed. "Maybe we should have. If you'd brought birth control with you, I know we would have. But that would have caused us self-discipline problems. I feel I'm already intimate with you."

"I know what you mean. Listen, since I'm going to land us, I'd better get in position."

"Ensign Waterford, take your duty station at the helm," Prescott said in a fake serious tone.

"Aye, aye Captain Barr," Priscilla said flashing a smile at Prescott.

Priscilla turned around pretending to be miffed. "I'm only an Ensign? I should be at least a Lieutenant Commander."

"Commander Waterford, take your duty station at the helm," Prescott repeated.

"Do you have your ready kit with you Commander Waterford?" Prescott asked.

"Yes. I trust Captain Barr has his as well."

"I do, Commander," Prescott replied.

Suddenly sounds of somebody walking through a jungle or forest was being broadcast all over the ship.

"What's that?" Prescott and Priscilla said at the same time.

Suddenly the entire ship was filled with a song called 'Calling Occupants of Interplanetary Craft' by the band Klaatu.

In your mind you have capacities, you know
To telepath messages through the vast unknown
Please close your eyes and concentrate
With every thought you think
Upon the recitation we're about to sing
Calling occupants of interplanetary craft
Calling occupants of interplanetary, most extraordinary craft
Calling occupants of interplanetary craft
Calling occupants of interplanetary craft
Calling occupants of interplanetary, most extraordinary craft
You've been observing our Earth
And we'd like to make
A contact with you
We are your friends
Calling occupants of interplanetary craft
Calling occupants of interplanetary, ultra-emissaries
We've been observing your Earth
And one night we'll make
A contact with you
We are your friends
Calling occupants of interplanetary, quite extraordinary craft
And please come in peace, we beseech you
Only our love we will teach them
Our Earth may never survive
So do come, we beg you
Please, interstellar policeman

Oh, won't you give us a sign
Give us a sign
That we've reached you
Oh do
With your mind you have ability to form
And transmit thought energy far beyond the norm
You close your eyes, you concentrate
Together, that's the way
To send the message we declare World Contact Day
Calling occupants of interplanetary craft
Calling occupants of interplanetary craft
Calling occupants of interplanetary, most extraordinary craft
Ah ah ah ahh
Ah ah ah ahh
Ah ah ah ahh
Calling occupants
Calling occupants
Calling occupants
Calling occupants
Calling occupants of interplanetary, most extraordinary craft

Chapter 15

Close Encounters of the Third Kind

Just as the song ended Prescott and Priscilla felt their iPhones vibrating.

"My FaceTime!" Prescott shouted out incredulous that a face, an alien face, was looking at him on his FaceTime feature on his iPhone.

"Mine too!" Priscilla sat, bolting from the helm toward Prescott.

They placed their iPhones side by side.

A pointed large greyish face with big slightly slanted black eyes was looking at them from their iPhones. The heard a voice, but it wasn't coming directly from their iPhones. The computer like voice was coming from inside their heads in understandable English.

"My name is Smiling Eyes. We've been tracking you since we received a signal beacon from the ship shortly after you left Earth. Please tell me your names."

Prescott and Priscilla were in such an excited state they could barely hold their iPhones up.

As the captain designate Prescott took the initiative, but found he couldn't get the words out. Priscilla came to his rescue.

"My name is Priscilla Waterford," Priscilla said shakily talking into her iPhone.

Prescott followed her lead.

"My name is Prescott Barr," Prescott said talking into his iPhone.

"We will bring you in. We've made arrangements for you to rest when you arrive. I know you have a thousand questions. There are many questions we have for you. We will have plenty of time to talk. Just relax. Please put your phones down and buckle yourselves in the chairs. The landing might be a bit bumpy."

Prescott and Priscilla were trembling in delirious happiness as they felt the saucer suddenly surge forward, then stall, then slowly start descending.

They went to the alien chairs in front of helm and navigation and buckled themselves in as directed with seat belts that looked like those you would find in the seat of any car on Earth.

Prescott was having some minor difficulty and discomfiture with his knees crammed under the console. Because of their weight loss they were able to fit themselves in.

Prescott and Priscilla arms were extended holding hands squeezing tight as they felt the saucer touch the ground and come to a shuddering stop.

Prescott and Priscilla unbuckled their seat belts as Priscilla grabbed her iPad from the top of the conn placing it in her large purse that was strapped across her body. Without a word they got out of their chairs as they heard the hatch door opening and the ramp extending.

Instinctively Prescott and Priscilla stood together huddled holding hands turning toward and looking at the bridge entrance to the corridor.

Prescott was glad they had decided not to bring weapons with them. Not that they would have used them and not that they would have done any good.

"Hello?" Came a voice coming from down the corridor.

A humanoid looking individual like the same one they'd just seen on their iPhones entered the bridge followed by two others.

"Welcome to Serpo, Prescott Barr and Priscilla Waterford. My name is Smiling Eyes. We've already met in a way."

Prescott and Priscilla relaxed and wave of well-being washed over them for some reason. They realized they might as well relax since they were 38 light years from Earth.

Prescott impulsively blurted out, "Klaatu barada nikto."

Smiling Eyes stared at him for a moment, then tilted its head up and emitted a loud rhythmic humming sound.

Priscilla cast a glance at Prescott, then asked Smiling Eyes, ""How were you able to speak to us on our iPhones?"

"We'll have plenty of time to discuss those things. Please, come with me. We've arranged a reception for you in the town hall."

Priscilla and Prescott noticed Smiling Eyes didn't move his, or her, mouth yet they could hear him or her clearly.

The voice Priscilla and Prescott heard in their minds coming from Smiling Eyes had a neutral computer sound to it.

They followed Smiling Eyes down the corridor and walked down the ramp to a group of about thirty to forty Greys all looking like Smiling Eyes. They were all about the same height some a little taller and some a little shorter.

The brightness of the day temporarily blinded Prescott and Priscilla until they took out their sunglasses from their ready kits and put them on.

The sky was blue same as on Earth. Two suns were visible one looking like Earth's sun in size and another one considerably smaller further in the distance but still visible.

The air was like the air on Earth. The gravity pull was the same.

The saucer had landed in an open area at the outskirts of a town or city.

The surrounding landscape looked arid like a desert without vegetation. It was hot.

Prescott removed the thermometer he had in his ready kit checked the temperature. "It's 103 degrees Fahrenheit Priscilla," Prescott said. "The humidity is low," Prescott added. "Let's put on our slouch hats and apply sunscreen."

Prescott and Priscilla took their slouch hats and sunscreen from the ready kits and applied the sunscreen on the faces and necks as the Greys watched wondering why they were doing that.

"Why do you place liquid on your skin and place a cover over your head?" Smiling Eyes inquired.

"To protect against your suns," Priscilla answered.

"I understand," Smiling Eyes said. "Our suns are intense."

"If I may ask are you male or female?" Priscilla asked Smiling Eyes, noticing all of the Greys appeared to be the same anatomically and appeared to be dressed alike with no apparent gender demarcations.

"Female," Smiling Eyes replied.

"How do you tell the difference?" Prescott asked.

"We just do. Let's not talk shop as you say," Smiling Eyes said. "Please, come with me to the banquet room in the town hall. We've arranged a dinner in your honor."

Prescott and Priscilla heard a strange loud humming sound coming from the crowd like an orchestra tuning up for a concert interspersed with sharp tonal sounds. It was somewhat grating to hear. The Greys who were greeting them seemed happy and were waving their elongated hands with four fingers in circular motions.

"Look at that," Priscilla said to Prescott pointing to a tall structure that hovered over the town.

A large tower conspicuous because of its height compared to the other buildings was standing in what appeared to be the town square.

"It looks like a cross between an electrical tower and university clock tower you'd see on Earth," Prescott noted. "Something like a reflecting device is on top of it. Wonder what it is."

The town or village seemed small. The road including all the streets intersecting with it were dirt as they walked to the town square.

Dust was kicking up as they walked on the dirt road. Dust from a dirt road was the last thing Prescott and Priscilla expected to see from aliens who could travel the galaxy at beyond the speed of light in incredible spaceships using incredible technology.

After walking for about a quarter of a mile Prescott and Priscilla followed Smiling Eyes and her entourage into the large building in the middle of town, which they'd observed and commented on from a distance.

The excited humming sound from the crowd following them now up to around sixty or seventy Greys kept up unabated. Prescott and Priscilla were getting used to the sound now.

Prescott and Priscilla followed Smiling Eyes into a large open area like a dining hall.

Ten long tables with a buffet table in the center greeted them. There was an eleventh and larger table right next to the buffet table although it only had four chairs.

Smiling Eyes guided Prescott and Priscilla to this table.

"Please sit here," Smiling Eyes gestured as Prescott and Priscilla sat down.

Smiling Eyes took a chair as did an unnamed Grey.

"This is Mind Healer," Smiling Eyes said.

Mind Healer waved its hand in a circular motion that Prescott and Priscilla mimicked. Prescott and Priscilla discerned this was how the Greys greeted each other.

Two Greys brought plates of food and placed them in front of Prescott and Priscilla.

"I hope you like the food," Smiling Eyes said. "This dish is what you would call a soup stew like jambalaya from Louisiana."

Prescott and Priscilla turned and looked at each other in surprise, then at Smiling Eyes.

"How can you possibly know about jambalaya and Louisiana?" Prescott asked.

Smiling Eyes let out a high-pitched sound while tilting her head upward.

"What did you just do?" Priscilla wanted to know.

"I laughed," Smiling Eyes replied.

Prescott had heard the Hank Williams song Jambalaya. Prescott deduced that jambalaya is a food dish as well as a song title.

Without waiting for Smiling Eyes to answer the question about jambalaya and Louisiana Prescott and Priscilla each took a bite of their stew or soup or whatever it was.

Prescott lifted his fork and spoon combination eating utensil to his mouth and took a bite.

"It's not bad," Prescott said to Smiling Eyes, diplomatically fibbing, as he chewed what to him at first tasted like spiced up bitter broccoli.

Priscilla tentatively put her fork spoon to her mouth and took a bite.

"Delicious," she said with sincerity, taking a second quick bite as Prescott looked at her in surprise wondering if she really liked it, or was being polite.

Prescott and Priscilla were feeling giddy like they'd both consumed half a bottle of wine. They were smiling at each other feeling goodwill and love from their surroundings.

Prescott and Priscilla were on a Grey induced high.

Since Prescott was feeling quite relaxed and congenial, he took a second bite. It wasn't so bad after all, Prescott decided as he chewed with gusto and decided he liked it. By the time Prescott had taken his third bite he was sold on it.

Smiling Eyes was looking at Prescott and Priscilla.

"I'm glad you like it," Smiling Eyes said.

"How did you manage to get that song to play in the ship when we were approaching Serpo?" Priscilla wanted to know.

"We'd heard you playing that song and we decided it would be a way for us to greet you because we recorded it and played it back through what you would call the ship's sound or stereo system. I like the words, if I understand them correctly. I like the title 'Calling Occupants of Interplanetary Craft'.

We were able to monitor you real time as you say. Our transmission beam uses a similar method like the gravity propulsion that moves our ships allowing the transmissions to arrive faster than the speed of light.

Nothing can travel faster than the speed of light and we are bound by that limitation the same as humans are, but as you know firsthand, we found a workaround to travel faster than the speed of light without violating Einstein. We know about Einstein we had our own scientists like him. Our transmission beam can travel even faster than our spaceships.

We recorded everything you said and did on your trip and it has been transmitting to us from the ship you were on since it left Area 51."

"You know about Area 51?" Prescott asked Smiling Eyes in some disbelief.

"For many of your decades we've been recording every conversation that occurred in and near the craft you were on. We've accumulated quite a library you could say, or quite a data base. It has also allowed us to perfect our translation devices. There are other ships from our planet you have in hangars including Hangars 6 and 7."

"The Sport Model?" Prescott asked, then adding, "And the Executive Model? The one parked outside of town?"

"Yes, the Sport Model and the Executive Model parked outside of town," Smiling Eyes verified.

"We've managed to learn English well between listening to the Americans and the British and researching books from what you call online files. We are working on learning other Earth languages too, but we understand English the best. Our Russian is also fluent because they've had several of our ships for many of your years too.

Chinese, or Mandarin, is hard because we had to convert to a new word formulation structure using root characters instead of letters. Mandarin characters are like ours in some ways conceptually.

Russian and English are from more similar language families, even though their alphabets are different.

Hebrew uses a script without vowels and reads right to left instead of left to right like English and other languages. It's been a challenging task for me."

"That must mean the British, the Chinese, the Russians and the Israelis have at least one of your ships too," Prescott stated.

"Yes, they do," Smiling Eyes confirmed.

"How did you manage to lose so many of your saucers?" Prescott asked surprised at his own directness with a host who was doing her best to be hospitable.

Prescott was feeling no pain.

"Errors were made," Smiling Eyes replied without taking offense. "Errors in procedure that have since been corrected."

"Try the liquid refreshment," Smiling Eyes suggested to Priscilla changing the subject. "We tried to make it similar to your cranberry juice."

Priscilla put the glass to her mouth and took a sip.

"Not bad. Tastes more like apple juice than cranberry juice, but close enough," she said as she swallowed it all.

Prescott followed and gulped his down. They were both thirsty partly because the Grey's version of jambalaya was spicy and partly because the dining room was warm though they felt a slight breeze as if it was coming from an unseen fan perhaps set up for their benefit.

A Grey standing near the buffet table came over and refilled each of their glasses.

Prescott and Priscilla noticed the dining hall and all ten tables were full of dozens of Greys who were going back and forth to the buffet table. Yet the clamor of the humming sound had gone away.

"I don't hear the other people anymore," Priscilla commented.

"I could tell the sound of our language is difficult for you to listen to so I put their voices on mute for you," Smiling Eyes told Priscilla.

Prescott was finishing up the Grey's version of jambalaya, which he now liked very much.

"Put the voices on mute?" Prescott said with curiosity. "How is it you can talk to me and Priscilla without moving your mouth, or what I think is your mouth?"

"It is a form of telepathic communication that your brains have too, you just don't know how to use it yet. I'm sure eventually your scientists will figure it out. Yes, I have a mouth as you can see because I'm using it to eat my food."

Prescott wasn't sure if Smiling Eyes was being sarcastic, or just stating a fact. Prescott felt foolish for asking a dumb question. Prescott decided Smiling Eyes was stating a fact and didn't seem like the sarcastic type, although she could laugh.

Smiling Eyes' mouth seemed to expand to a larger proportion of her face when she took a bite and then her mouth went back to its original small and barely perceptible configuration.

The euphoric mood Prescott was feeling made his feeling of embarrassment a fleeting one.

Prescott boldly continued his line of questioning.

"You, meaning your people, usually communicate verbally then? I mean all those sounds I heard that I assume is your language. Can you talk both verbally and mentally, or telepathically?"

"Yes, we can," Smiling eyes answered. "We mostly talk verbally because it is easier and it is considered impolite for two people to talk using telepathy with each other while a third person is present. If two people are talking alone it's fine to use telepathy. But usually only close friends use telepathy to talk."

The other Grey had remained silent during the conversation.

Smiling Eyes decided to bring Mind Healer into the conversation.

"We know from your conversations how you stole what you call the Executive Model saucer you used to fly to us and we know you are having mental conflicts about betraying your friends and country. The concept of a country is a difficult one for us to grasp because we have no such divisions on Serpo.

Mind Healer is a gifted psychiatrist to use your terminology. He has studied your situation and we have made arrangements for you to visit his office tomorrow. I understand saying tomorrow could be a misleading for you since we really never have a night time more like a period of dusk, but we will let you know. Our day is about 30 of your hours. We won't force you, but I believe Mind Healer can help you."

Prescott and Priscilla looked at each other and nodded their heads.

"Does that gesture mean yes?" Mind Healer asked.

"Yes, it means yes," Prescott and Prescott said almost simultaneously.

"Excellent," Smiling Eyes exclaimed looking around at the group gathered to honor Prescott's and Priscilla's arrival. "Everyone is about finished eating. We have prepared a show for you with dancing and music. I enjoy your classical music especially Bach. We have chants that sound like Bach."

"I brought a CD of what are called Gregorian Chants," Priscilla said, her eyes flashing. "I didn't play any of them during the voyage so you didn't hear them," Priscilla said.

"I look forward to listening to those chants. Do either of you need to refresh yourselves?" Smiling Eyes asked.

"You mean use the restroom? Yes, I do," Prescott confirmed, breaking into a wide smile.

"Why do I feel so good?" Prescott asked Smiling Eyes and Mind Healer and then turning to Priscilla. "Do you feel good babe?" Prescott asked.

"I do babe," Priscilla agreed. "I feel really good."

"You can blame me," Smiling Eyes replied. "We put some tranquilizers in your food supervised by Mind Healer. Don't worry there will be no deleterious effects from our medication. When you arrived, I was able to project some telegraphic suggestions onto you to help keep you happy. Or make you happy."

"Can you hypnotize people Smiling Face? I mean Smiling Eyes, sorry. I can. I hypnotized a coworker Susan."

"I remember hearing you talk about that adventure with Priscilla," Smiling Eyes said as she tilted her head upward again letting out another high-pitched sound of laughter.

Smiling Eyes told a curious Mind Healer by private telepathy she'd fill him in on the Prescott and Susan caper later.

Prescott and Priscilla were grinning like Cheshire cats.

"I'm feeling good. Are you feeling good Pres?" Priscilla asked, laughing. "I'm feeling good. Are you feeling good Pris?" Prescott asked back, laughing with her their heads bumping as they slumped into each other.

They leaned over holding each other in a semi-state of inebriation and intoxication as both Smiling Eyes and Mind Healer tilted their heads up and emitted a high-pitched sound of laughter.

"I got to ask you a question Smiling Eyes," Prescott said his head spinning from the tranquilizers provided by Mind Healer, "then I must go pee. You live in what looks to me to be simple villages. Your roads aren't paved and your homes and I guess businesses and other buildings appear to be of simple basic construction. I was imaging you'd have flying cars and sleek buildings made from the same material your flying saucers are made from."

Smiling Eyes' small slit of a mouth was formed into an imperceptible smile on her face.

"We'll talk about that another time. Why don't you go urinate now? The show is about to begin. Mind Healer will take you to the restroom."

"Do you have unisex restrooms?" Priscilla asked. "I'm asking because that's the way it is on your spaceship, unless crews are only one gender. We think the last crew was both genders."

"Our restrooms are unisex as you call it," Smiling Eyes confirmed.

Smiling Eyes looked at Mind Healer. "Take Prescott to the restroom."

Prescott began walking with Mind Healer, then spun around looking at Smiling Eyes.

"Hey, you've got to fill me in on how the shower works. I can walk through the curtain, but I can't see through it. How the heck is that done? Priscilla saw me naked because the shower curtain shorted out while I was looking for a towel to dry myself with," Prescott slurred.

Smiling Eyes tilted her head up and emitted a high-pitched sound of laughter once more.

"I need to go too," Priscilla said, as she began to follow Prescott and Mind Healer to the restroom.

Then Priscilla had a question of her own. "Do you have last names?" she asked Smiling Eyes.

Smiling Eyes didn't reply as Priscilla stumbled forward like a punch drunk and ran through the crowd of Greys assembled in their honor to catch up with Prescott and Mind Healer.

After the banquet and show was over it can be said that a good time was had by all.

Priscilla was stirring in her bed as she opened her eyes trying to get her sea legs. She slowly set up in bed noticing it was small and close to the floor. Prescott was in a bed right next to hers snoring.

Priscilla slowly stretched reaching out and pushing at Prescott's arm. The snoring ceased.

Prescott's feet extended over the edge of the bed a little. He still had on his shoes and clothes like she did.

Priscilla got up. She was trying to remember how she and Prescott ended up in this room, unless it was part of a larger structure like a house.

Priscilla opened a curtain that looked like and whose material felt like any curtain on Earth and looked out the window. The sunshine streaming in was a shade too bright and she quickly shut the curtain.

She momentarily panicked looking around for her purse and ready kit. Relieved, she saw both of them draped over a small chair. Prescott's ready kit was draped over another small chair.

Then she saw all four pieces of their luggage, several cases of food and clothing were neatly stacked in a corner.

Priscilla saw a door. Hoping it was a bathroom Priscilla opened the door and it was.

Priscilla exited the bathroom and decided it was time that Prescott got up.

Priscilla sat down on Prescott's bed and began moving him around. "Wake up sleepyhead. Wake up, Prescott," Priscilla said, who was now vigorously shaking him back and forth.

"What's going on?" Prescott asked opening his eyes.

"Time to get up," Priscilla said.

"Where are we?" Prescott said as he sat up rubbing his eyes.

"The bathroom is over there," Priscilla said, pointing to the small door.

Without saying a word Prescott got up and entered the bathroom.

Priscilla checked out her purse and ready kit. Everything was there including her iPad.

"What time is it?" Prescott asked as he emerged from the bathroom.

"My iPhone says it's 5:34 pm, but that doesn't mean much. I wonder how long we were asleep?"

"Probably ten or twelve hours. We were tired. Last thing I remember was Smiling Face introducing us to the crowd on the podium before they began their chanting."

"Her name is Smiling Eyes, not Smiling Face. Why can't you get her name right?"

"I don't know," Prescott said yawning. "She's very nice. So is what's his face Mind Reader."

"Mind Healer, Prescott. His name is Mind Healer. Come on, get with it. It might be considered a serious social faux pas to forget somebody's name."

"It wouldn't be the first time I've done that," Prescott said under his breath as he checked out his ready kit seeing that everything was there.

"They brought us our luggage from the saucer and our clothes and other items," Priscilla told Prescott, pointing to the corner.

"That was nice of them," Prescott said.

Priscilla took her iPad from her purse and sat down at the diminutive desk in the corner of the room just being able to tuck her legs and knees in under the desk.

"What are you doing?" Prescott asked sitting back down on the bed and lying down flat.

"I'm going to begin my journal now. I'm already a day behind schedule. Quite a momentous day yesterday, wasn't it?"

Prescott didn't answer.

Priscilla turned around and saw that Prescott was drifting off to sleep again.

"Don't go to sleep!" Priscilla said.

"Then get me a cup of coffee," Prescott advised as he rolled over turning his back to her.

Priscilla turned back to her iPad and began writing in her journal.

Day 1 – This is Priscilla Waterford. Arrived at Serpo on estimated Earth day December 26, 20XX, which is 36 days since we launched from Area 51 on November 21, 20XX. The exact time of this journal entry is unknown because of the difference in the length of the day here. My iPhone now reads 5:45 pm so it could be 5:45 pm Pacific Standard Time on the evening of December 27, 20XX. My traveling companion Prescott Barr and I were asleep for an indeterminate amount of time. I woke up about fifteen minutes ago. I just realized Prescott and I missed Christmas.

1. Prescott and I were automatically guided in when we reached the atmosphere of Serpo. We were met by a delegation of aliens I will refer to as the Greys. As was the case with Colonel Smith Greys is easier to say than Ebens or Serpens. The two Greys who were our primary contacts is a female named Smiling Eyes and a male named Mind Healer.
2. They were able to communicate with us telepathically and in understandable good English. The voices used by Smiling Eyes and Mind Healer sound computer generated. They administered tranquilizers to us in our food without our permission and told us after the fact. They promised there would be no deleterious effects and as far as I can determine there haven't been. Prescott and I were tense and nervous, but also enthralled at having successfully landed on Serpo. The first words spoken by humans on Serpo were by Prescott. He said that quote from the movie The Day The Earth Stood Still 'Klaatu barada nikto'. There's one for the history books.
3. I'm afraid Prescott and I were for lack of a better description drunk by the time the banquet ended. As Prescott said as we were being escorted home (in a manner of speaking), "We're wasted, but it's not our fault." That is true, it wasn't. The tranquilizers or whatever the Greys gave us did keep us calm and helped us enjoy the food and show they had gone to some bother to arrange for us. We didn't wake up with a hangover. I didn't. I don't think Prescott did either. He is tired but that's because he's tired.

4. They gave us a banquet and Broadway show so to speak in our honor. The food wasn't bad. The banquet and show were all enjoyable, even if the show was a bit tedious. This is interesting Smiling Eyes said one of the dishes they served us is similar to jambalaya. The Greys know a lot about Earth and are able to receive transmissions from their ships that are in custody on Earth from the USA, Russia, China, Israel and the UK.
5. It is impossible for my travel companion Prescott Barr and I to tell the difference between male and female Greys, but for the record Smiling Eyes told us they have gender. Smiling Eyes is female and Mind Healer is male. I wrote that already. We've only been on Serpo for one day so we may learn to tell the difference between males and females.
6. They dress almost identically and are between three and a half to four feet in height on average. We saw a couple of Greys yesterday who might have been two and a half feet tall and a couple who may have been four and a half feet tall. They have their variety of taller and shorter people like humans.
7. Their skin color has a greyish hue. Their bodies are elongated and their limbs are proportionally different from human beings. Their upper arms and lower arm and upper legs and lower legs are the same length. They have a small chest cavity. They have large black eyes that bend around at an angle or slant wrapping around the sides of their faces a little. They have what look like slits for mouths and ears. When they were eating at the banquet their mouths seemed to expand in size to accommodate the spoon forks they use, then their mouths returned to their original small size.
8. They lift their heads up when laughing. It is a sound with a high pitch. Their language sounds like discordant humming. Smiling Eyes was somehow able to filter it out of our conscious awareness last night at the banquet. She undid the filter during the show so we could hear it. One of their chants sounded a little like Bach.

9. Their heads are disproportionally large compared to their bodies, which from what Prescott and I can see are all thin. We didn't see any obese Greys, or haven't seen any obese Greys yet. We haven't seen any children yet, unless some of the shorter Greys who greeted us yesterday are children.
10. Instead of modern cities the town we're in has dirt roads and simple buildings. There is one large tall building that seems to serve an unknown purpose. The other large building in town is the one where they held the banquet for us last night. The building we're being put up in seems solid. I think the Greys have the air conditioning on for us because it is pleasantly cool. Yesterday we measured the temperature at 103 degrees F.
11. The air is breathable and the sky is blue and the gravity pull is the same. They have two suns. The larger sun Zeta 2 Reticuli looks to be the same size as our sun, or put another way their planet Serpo is about the same distance from their larger sun as Earth is from its sun. The other sun Zeta 1 Reticuli is about a seventh of the size in the sky as Zeta 2 Reticuli. It is much further away.
12. The topography of where we're at is similar to the desert part of Nevada arid without any visible vegetation.

My hand is getting tired now from keyboarding and I want to get Prescott up. He fell asleep again. I plan to summarize the end of Day 2 later today.

Priscilla sat back in the chair moving her neck around in a circle.

Priscilla got up from the desk and walked over to Prescott, who was sleeping. Priscilla went into the bathroom, took a small glass on the sink, engaged the faucet with a wave of her hand, filled the glass with cold water and brought it over to Prescott whose face was looking up at the ceiling.

Priscilla tipped the glass and poured a little cold water on Prescott's face.

Prescott shot up in the bed shaking his head wiping the water from his face.

"What did you do that for?" Prescott asked, displeased.

"To get you up. I've already made my Day 1 journal entry and I would like you to read and check it and edit it if necessary. Here we are Day 2 on a planet 38 light years from Earth and you're sleeping in. Merry Christmas two days late."

Prescott laughed at himself and at the way Priscilla described things.

"Now that you put it that way, you're right. I'll consider that my morning shower. By all means let's get going. I'm sure Smiley Face – sorry, Smiling Eyes – will be along soon. A late Merry Christmas to you too Pris."

Priscilla lay down on her bed as Prescott checked several boxes looking for his shaving cream and razor and found them.

As Prescott was shaving Priscilla heard a knock on the door. She opened the door. It was Smiling Eyes.

"Good morning," Smiling Eyes said. "May I come in?" she asked.

"Good morning," Priscilla replied back. "Please come in."

"Smiling Eyes is here," Priscilla called out to Prescott who was still in the bathroom shaving.

Prescott stuck his head of the door his face half-shaved. "Good morning Smiley Face. Thanks for arranging to have our luggage and supplies brought to our room. Be there in a minute."

Priscilla shook her head. "Sorry, he knows your name is Smiling Eyes."

"Did you sleep well?" Smiling Eyes asked Priscilla.

"Prescott and I were out like a light."

"Out like a light," Smiling Eyes repeated. "I understand. An idiom. Out like a light. Very good."

Smiling Eyes tilted her head upward letting out a high-pitched sound of laughter.

"I know you and Prescott have many questions and one of our top scholars Knowing Much will give you a briefing later today. Let's have breakfast. You and Prescott must be hungry."

"We are," Priscilla confirmed.

Prescott emerged from the bathroom freshly shaven.

"Smiling Eyes is going to take us to breakfast," Priscilla said.

"I'm starved," Prescott said. "If you pay for breakfast, I'll cover the tip."

Smiling Eyes appeared to have a puzzled look on her face. Then she tilted her head upward letting out a high-pitched sound of laughter.

Priscilla and Prescott put sunscreen on their faces and grabbed their slouch hats and sunglasses. As the stepped out of the building they saw it was like a quonset hut in design and size located in the center of town.

A strong wind was blowing and gusting requiring Prescott and Priscilla to secure their slouch hats to their heads. The two suns were beating down as always.

Smiling Eyes led Prescott and Priscilla back to the same dining hall where the banquet had been held.

A Grey approached them holding a large tray and placed plates in front of Prescott and Priscilla.

Each plate had on it what looked like two buttermilk pancakes drenched in butter and syrup, two eggs over easy, two strips of bacon and two sausage links.

"How did you make this?" Priscilla asked Smiling Eyes in astonishment as Prescott was already using his fork spoon to scoop up a large bite of pancake.

Smiling Eyes was enjoying watching Prescott launch into his breakfast.

"We've been intercepting your transmissions and seen what you call commercials on your television and internet and this seems to be very important for your first nutrition of the day," Smiling Eyes explained.

"Studying your internet from our transmission beams has been especially valuable for us as an information and news source for learning about life on Earth. How do you like your food?"

"Very good," Prescott and Priscilla said.

"Would you like some of that liquid you've built shrines to all over your different cultures called Starbucks?" Smiling Eyes asked like a solicitous host. "This must be very important to your cultures."

Prescott swallowed the last of his buttermilk pancakes and said, "If you mean coffee, I take mine with two creamers and two sugars."

"Same for me," Priscilla chimed in. "I'll also take a glass of orange juice if you have it," Priscilla requested.

"We have orange juice," Smiling Eyes replied. "We are doing our best to approximate the Earth cuisine you are used to. I'll bring you both a cup of coffee and a glass of orange juice," Smiling Eyes said.

After breakfast Smiling Eyes guided Priscilla and Prescott to another room that looked like a small theatre. The seats were just large enough to accommodate them, although Prescott had to shift around until he was comfortable.

A Grey called Knowing Much gave Prescott and Priscilla a tour de force of the history of Serpo and its people. Many if not most of the questions they had were answered during this presentation. Knowing Much's English left a lot to be desired, but Smiling Eyes was there to correct any mistranslations and act as a monitor to clarify questions and answers.

They were left in awe.

After the presentation Smiling Eyes had a question for them.

"Would you still like to see Mind Healer? It's your choice. We know the mental anguish you are going through and I believe Mind Healer can help you."

"Yes," Prescott and Priscilla said in unison without hesitation.

After a light lunch Smiling Eyes participated in a mandatory ceremony lasting about one hour when all of the Greys went home to take a siesta. Prescott and Priscilla went to their assigned house and waited for Smiling Eyes to get them.

Smiling Eyes walked Prescott and Priscilla to Mind Healer's office not far from where they were staying.

"Hello," Mind Healer said. "I've cleared my schedule for you. Come in."

Smiling Eyes waited for them in the waiting room.

After Prescott's and Priscilla's appointment with Mind Healer was over Smiling Eyes took them on several tours.

Priscilla and Prescott returned to their assigned house mentally exhausted their heads spinning with all they had learned.

They were on a natural high.

"We've got to document Day 2 immediately," Priscilla said.

"Absolutely," Prescott agreed. "This time I'll key in this journal entry if you don't mind. You did a great job on Day 1 and it's only fair I do Day 2. You can edit of course."

"Agreed," Priscilla said as she lay down on her bed to rest. "I'm tired partly because of my period. I know you are tired too. I didn't finish Day 1, but let's look ahead. Start on Day 2."

Prescott tried to squeeze in the chair and put his legs under the desk. With some difficulty he was able to finally position himself where he could keyboard comfortably.

The iPad with the Day 1 journal entry in it was on top of the desk.

"I'd like to run things by you if you're up to it Priscilla. I've got a lot to document. You know what a day we've had."

"That will be fine," Priscilla said. "Don't hesitate to ask me."

He would follow the format Priscilla had established when she documented Day 1 in the journal including numbering the paragraphs.

Day 2 – This is Prescott Barr. The exact time of this journal entry is unknown because of the difference in the length of the day here. My iPhone now reads 11:35 pm so it could be 11:35 pm Pacific Standard Time on the evening of December 28, 20XX. This is a guess. Priscilla and I are slowly getting used to the Grey's time reference.

My traveling companion Priscilla Waterford and I attended a briefing today on the history of Serpo and its people. She is better qualified than I am to document what we learned, but because she is having a health issue, I am going to write down everything I can remember from the lecture that is not necessarily in chronological order. I will number different observations like Priscilla did.

I am also going to write everything down from several visits we made to various locations with Smiling Eyes as our guide. I apologize if I comingle what Knowing Much and Smiling Eyes said and did.

I will write down what comes to me including independent observations Priscilla and I have made. I wish I had a laptop to word process this. Priscilla will be validating everything that I write. This is going to take me awhile.

1. Knowing Much told me they will adhere to the agreement they have with MJ-12 and other similar Earth agencies not to discuss prior contact information with Earth authorities meaning Area 51, etc.
2. They once had an enemy from another planet that has been destroyed. Knowing Much didn't want to elaborate.
3. They've been monitoring Earth for two thousand years. Our years.
4. Their life span is between 250-300 years in Earth years. They are mortal like humans. Sometimes Greys are killed in air transport accidents. More about that later.
5. Their suns Zeta 1 Reticuli and Zeta 2 Reticuli do not set like our sun. There is daylight during their entire day, with the exception of a short time period where both suns hit the horizon. Zeta 1 Reticuli dips below the horizon for a time while Zeta 2 Reticuli sits on the horizon.
6. Knowing Much went over the Grey's alphabet with the equivalent English letters. This confirmed that our translations are basically correct.
7. Each town has a large tower that tells the Greys what activity they are to be doing. It's hard to explain unless you see it in action. It's like a clock and a sun dial. Sunlight is directed through a mirror to seven symbols carved into a long structure set up on the one non-dirt area in the town square. When light contacts symbol the Grey make a change to their routine. Each symbol means a specific work period at a specific time. A simplistic way to look at it is among other things it lets the Greys know when a siesta is to begin. The Greys don't sleep

eight hours straight like we do they take naps. The Grey's day is structured.

8. All the buildings looks like quonset huts. Some are larger than others. They are built of a durable material that looks like metal but feels like solid rubber to the touch. Lights are affixed to the walls and ceilings and can be controlled by a wave of the hand to turn them on and off and control the illumination. They use electricity same as we do that is extracted from the vacuum. We noticed this on the ship when the appliances we brought with us worked without an electrical power source.
9. It's hard for us to tell the Greys apart by age and sex. Priscilla and I observed there are a group of Greys who wear the same uniforms and are always walking around in pairs. Smiling Eyes told us they are the military. They perform police functions too. We have a sense they either don't have crime, or their crime rate is low.
10. Priscilla and I visited a greenhouse with Smiling Eyes where they grow food in soil. They have a watering system. They were growing vegetables similar to potatoes and tomatoes. They also have something like lettuce. They are vegetarians for the most part, but they do have meat eaters among them. They raise animals similar to cattle for that purpose located in another building we didn't visit. Smiling Eyes told us every town has their own greenhouse.
11. Smiling Eyes arranged for us to take a helicopter that is more like a flying car or a hovercraft with her over to a nearby town a few kilometers away to see a manufacturing plant. It was a lot of fun, but as noted sometimes flying cars have accidents like cars have accidents on Earth. I was joking with Smiling Eyes hoping the pilot's driver's license was up to date. She didn't realize I was joking and she had the driver show us his driving certification that serves as their driver's license.

    Everything they make is sealed with a melting method, or soldered in some way. We were amazed how efficient they manufacture furniture and certain appliances, which is what that particular plant made. It is mostly automated. I asked Smiling Eyes if automation caused any problems with their union workforce and she didn't understand. Finally, she realized I was joking and she finally got the joke and she let out that laugh she makes. It's good the Greys have a sense of humor. They are very quick witted.

They have several spacecraft manufacturing plants, but they are too far away for us to visit, unless Priscilla and I decide to stay on Serpo, which is looking more and more likely, if they will let us. I think they would. This is interesting. The plant we visited is a subcontractor to one of the spacecraft manufacturing plants. They don't use money. More on that later. We found out the Greys don't have refrigeration except for some of their manufacturing processes. That's why we couldn't find any on the saucer.

12. The temperature of the planet, at the center, stays between 93-degrees and 112-degrees Fahrenheit. They have clouds and occasional rain only during a brief seasonal period of their year, whatever that is exactly. The temperature in the northern and southern polar parts of the planet if you want to call it that averages 60 and 80-degrees F. Most of the Greys live near the center, or the equator of the planet. Most of the planet is uninhabited. They don't have oceans. They have lakes and rivers most of which are further north and further south from where we are. They also have forests which are further north and further south and ice caps at the top and bottom of Serpo like Earth.

13. They have a decentralized form of government like city states who coordinate together. They have regular meetings within each town like city council meeting. If I understood Smiling Eyes there is one city that functions as their capital, or world capital.

14. Their population is only 14.6 million spread over a planet about the size of Earth, concentrated in the center northern part of their planet Serpo. Smiling Eyes said most people have a mate who is preselected by some unknown council of people. Sounds like a group of matchmakers. They must be approved to reproduce and are told many children they can have. Priscilla and I haven't seen many children. Smiling Eyes said the children are in school or what we would call day care centers. They plan the birth of each child carefully.
15. They don't use money. Every Grey is issued what they needed. They don't have malls or stores. Instead they have distribution centers where they go to get what they need. I asked Smiling Eyes how do they know who got what and if people cheated. Smiling Eyes said a lot of our questions are answered in some mysterious briefing books she eluded to and didn't elaborate on. Maybe in their society the urge or quest for material goods has dissipated.
16. Priscilla asked me to include that if the vision that Karl Marx had about a classless society where he said 'from each according to his abilities, to each according to his needs' would ever be reached the Greys on Serpo have reached it.
17. The Greys are one ethnic group and have one language perhaps this allows for greater consensus.

    I am going to take a rest. I hope I can finish before I go to bed. Prescott took a ten-minute break, then resumed keying into the iPad.
18. We haven't noticed any bugs and we haven't asked. We haven't noticed any domestic animals such as dogs or cats or any wild animals. They raise cattle for beef I guess you could call it as noted in number 10.
19. The Greys have schools to train people in different skills for which they are best qualified.
20. They worship a Supreme Being. It appeared to be some sort of deity relating to the Universe. Knowing Much said more on this

would be provided later. Priscilla and I were and are confused on exactly what he meant. Smiling Eyes didn't respond to our questions either. They are tight lipped about that topic. They don't have lips ha ha.

21. Their music sounds like tonal rhythms and chanting. They are dancers who did elaborately choreographed dancing when we were at the banquet the first night we were here. Music is played using bells and drums. Some of it is nice. Smiling Eyes liked the Gregorian Chanting CD Priscilla brought with her. Priscilla let Smiling Eyes borrow her CD player. Priscilla asked me to note that Smiling Eyes is very fond of Bach and she likes Klaatu too. Both sound like their chants Bach more than Klaatu. Smiling Eyes said some of Klaatu's songs sounds like their chants.

22. They don't have entertainment like television or movies or video games. They have a simple society. It is completely the opposite of what Priscilla and I expected. It is counterintuitive as Priscilla says considering their technology. Go figure.

23. This is my last entry for Day 2. Mind Healer, the Grey psychiatrist or psychologist or therapist or whatever he is was helpful to Priscilla and myself. We explained, or rather he already knew, the mental conflicts and angst we've been having about stealing the saucer and flying to Serpo. Mind Healer gave us some medication to help us feel better. It is in pill form and he says it is non addicting. Priscilla and I are following the instructions. The meds are helping to keep us centered and anxiety free, for the most part.

24. Priscilla has approved what I've written because I read out everything to her and revised wording when necessary based on her input.

25. Priscilla just reminded me of one thing. Knowing Much was very interested in finding out how Priscilla was able to isolate Element 115 and release stable antimatter. We told Knowing Much and Smiling Eyes it was classified. They didn't object to that explanation.

Prescott shifted in the chair because his right leg was tingling.

"My right leg went asleep," Prescott said slowly getting up. "My knees hurt a little from having them crammed underneath the small desk."

"You did it, honey," Priscilla said, smiling at Prescott, who laid down on his small bed right next to hers. His hands were tired from furious keyboarding.

"It seems the Greys want us to be together in the same room or the same house," Prescott commented. "I think this house or whatever you want to call it only has one room and one bathroom. Priscilla, there is something we need to discuss."

"Way ahead of you. Let me guess. Asking Smiling Eyes if we can stay on Serpo."

"Yeah, how did you know?" he asked.

"Because we already talked about it earlier when you were writing, remember?"

"I guess we did. I think we need to formally ask Serpo through Smiling Eyes for asylum. I think the odds of our beating the rap on Earth for stealing the saucer are nil. You and I knew what we were doing. You know it was explained to us during our Area 51 onboarding briefing that what we did is a death penalty offense."

He let out a long sigh feeling depressed despite Mind Healer's potent anti-anxiety medication.

"I know," she said quietly. "We made a poor decision."

Prescott started to chuckle.

"What are you laughing about?" Priscilla asked.

"I was just thinking they bugged the saucer. No wonder Smiling Face, I mean Smiling Eyes, has been laughing so much. She must know everything we did on the saucer."

"And everything we didn't do," Priscilla said, wryly grinning at Prescott. "They've probably bugged this house."

She stood up. "It looks like it is getting dark. That'd be a first."

Priscilla pulled back the curtain. "It is dusk, Prescott. Let's go outside."

They went outside.

"Look how pretty the pink sky is Pres. It reminds me of the old sailor's wisdom pink clouds at night, sailor's delight."

Prescott and Priscilla held each other enjoying a cool breeze as two cops walked by.

They could see a thin slice of Zeta 1 Reticuli just above the horizon.

A knock on the door rousted Prescott and Priscilla from a deep sleep. Prescott staggered to the door and opened it part way.

"Good morning," Smiling Eyes said. "Is this a bad time?"

"We're still in bed. I mean in separate beds. We were sleeping."

Smiling Eyes tilted her head upward letting out a high-pitched sound of laughter.

"I'll come back in two of your hours," she said. "Unless you'd like more time to sleep?"

"Two hours works," he said. "See you then."

Prescott and Priscilla were going over the petition they would present to Smiling Eyes.

"That about says it all," she said. "This shouldn't come as a surprise to them. I can get used to living here. Better than the alternative of returning to Earth and being executed, or spending the rest of our lives in a harsh federal penitentiary."

"You said it," he agreed, reviewing the petition he and Priscilla had jointly crafted.

A knock on the door indicated Smiling Eyes was in the house.

Prescott looked at his iPhone. "She's right on time two hours exactly."

"Punctual as always," Priscilla added.

He opened the door and invited Smiling Eyes in.

"Hi," Priscilla said to Smiling Eyes as Smiling Eyes bent her head in acknowledgement.

Prescott gestured to the desk chair and turned it around so it faced the beds.

"Please sit down, Smiling Eyes. Priscilla and I have something important to discuss with you."

"As do I," Smiling Eyes replied as she sat down in the chair.

"You go first," Priscilla remarked.

"No, please let me know what's on your mind," Smiling Eyes said.

"It's like this," Prescott began sitting on the side of his bed. "If Priscilla and I go back to Earth we'll be facing serious criminal charges up to and including the death penalty. We have prepared a petition formally asking your government to grant us asylum to remain on Serpo for the rest of our lives."

"I see," Smiling Eyes said.

"What do you think?" Priscilla asked.

"I think you should hear my offer first," Smiling Eyes said. "We know about your predicament and the legal charges you would be facing by the United States government because you took the spacecraft from Area 51 without authorization."

"We stole the saucer," Prescott emphasized so Smiling Eyes would have no doubt as to the serious nature of the charges that would be levied against them.

"Yes, you stole the saucer," Smiling Eyes said. "But it is still our saucer. We never relinquished official control over its ownership. The saucer is still the property of Serpo and its people. You returned the saucer to its rightful owners."

"That's right. We did, didn't we?" Prescott said slapping his thigh in glee.

Priscilla bounced off her bed and sat down next to Prescott facing Smiling Eyes who was sitting in the chair.

"Legally speaking we have a case," Priscilla said, clapping her hands together and hugging Prescott.

"Can you get us a good lawyer?" Prescott asked Smiling Eyes, who looked at him with her large black eyes for a few seconds, then tilted her head upward again letting out a high-pitched sound of laughter.

"That's not necessary," Smiling Eyes said. "We have an idea. When I say we I mean the government of Serpo. I am the designated spokesperson. We feel this would be an excellent time to open formal diplomatic relations with all of the countries of Earth."

"What are you proposing?" Priscila asked.

"You and Prescott and I return to Earth together. We can travel at what you call Warp 7 and arrive in 21 Earth days. Technicians are already doing systems upgrades to the saucer. Its technology is a little dated. We would make the establishment of diplomatic relations contingent upon all charges being dropped against you both."

Priscilla squealed with excitement and Prescott let out a yip of joy.

"What if they don't agree?" Priscilla asked.

"Then we grant you asylum and we all return to Serpo and you may live the remainder of your lives here."

Priscilla and Prescott jumped up and rushed over to Smiling Eyes and began hugging her.

"What big eyes you have," Prescott said as he hugged Smiling Eyes.

"Your head is even bigger than your eyes," Priscilla said, laughing, as she hugged Smiling Eyes repeatedly.

"I take it your answer is yes," Smiling Eyes said as they continued hugging her.

Chapter 16

Hope has Wings

A large crowd was gathering on the open dirt field where the saucer was parked. Large klieg lights had been set up around the perimeter and illuminated the newly upgraded saucer.

A choral group was chanting. Another group was dancing around the choral group swaying to the rhythms.

"You checked the room?" Prescott asked Priscilla again.

"Yes. Three times. Everything was packed. I did a final look around including the bathroom and under the beds. We have everything. I made sure to put the iPad with our journal in my purse," Priscilla stated, patting the large purse that was draped around her body.

Smiling Eyes and Mind Healer were standing together humming with some high-level Serpo government representatives going over final details.

Mind Healer would be accompanying them. Come to find out Mind Healer was a first-rate military pilot when he wasn't practicing psychiatry in civilian life.

It was getting dark. The sky was turning from a deep dark blue to pink. The two suns were setting. Stars were twinkling. A slight wind was kicking up.

Smiling Eyes walked over to Prescott and Priscilla who were waiting ecstatically by the ramp leading into the saucer.

"Please come with me. They want to bid you goodbye. I will act as translator."

Smiling Eyes led Prescott and Priscilla to a row of chairs in front of a small temporary podium. Two larger chairs were conspicuously placed in the middle of the row in deference to the larger size of Prescott and Priscilla. An official looking Grey walked to the podium.

Smiling Eyes sat down beside Prescott and Priscilla readying herself to translate and communicate the speech telepathically.

"Welcome. We are gathered here today to honor two visitors from Earth Prescott Barr and Priscilla Waterford who journeyed all the way from Earth to visit us."

A loud humming sound began emitting from the crowd as the Greys including Smiling Eyes began rotating their four-fingered hands in quick circular motions.

"We also wish to honor our number one diplomat Smiling Eyes Drumdordrumdor and the well-respected doctor and military pilot Mind Healer Laolellaolel. These two brave pioneers will go with Prescott and Priscilla to Earth to hopefully establish diplomatic relations."

Priscilla whispered to Prescott, "The Greys do have last names."

"We wish you all a safe journey and a successful outcome," the Grey leader said.

Another loud humming sound emitted from the crowd as the Greys began rotating their four-fingered hands in quick circular motions once more.

The officious looking Grey leader stepped down from the podium and shook Prescott's and Priscilla's hands in accordance with Earth custom.

Prescott, Priscilla, Smiling Eyes and Mind Healer all approached the ramp leading to the inside of the saucer. They all turned around. Prescott and Priscilla were emulating Smiling Eyes and Mind Healer and were rotating their hands in circular motions waving back to the waving crowd.

Then they all walked inside the saucer as the ramp retracted and the door closed shut.

All four walked down the corridor to the bridge.

Mind Healer took the newly refurbished captain's chair as Smiling Eyes took the helm.

"Would you like to sit at navigation Priscilla?" Smiling Eyes asked.

"Sure!" Priscilla responded delighted. "You know how the helm and navigation work?"

"All Greys, or Ebens, as you call us are trained in the basics of spaceflight."

Priscilla slid herself into the navigator's chair.

"Why don't you sit in the first officer's chair?" Mind Healer said to Prescott telepathically.

"I'd be honored," Prescott said as he sat down fitting himself into the first officer's chair next to the captain's chair. Luckily the nine pounds he'd lost since leaving Earth made it possible.

"Tell me Captain," Prescott asked Mind Healer. "Is there a main engineering section on this vessel?"

"No, all Greys are trained in basic engineering. It's part of our educational curriculum."

"Did you hear that Priscilla?" Prescott called out. "Just like we thought they don't have a main engineering section."

"Secure your safety belts," Mind Healer ordered everyone.

"Ready on the thrusters," Mind Healer said to Smiling Eyes.

"Ready!" Smiling Eyes confirmed

"Engage!" Mind Healer said.

The glowing saucer began to lift upwards wobbling a little.

Then it gained some altitude to fifteen feet, hovered momentarily, and shot up into the night sky.

"Course set," Priscilla said, looking over at Smiling Eyes, who Priscilla thought for a moment winked at her.

"Ready for second thruster," Smiling Eyes said.

"Engage!" Mind Healer said.

"Go to third thruster and take us out," Mind Healer said to Smiling Eyes.

The saucer quickly left the upper atmosphere of Serpo and was headed to Earth.

Mind Healer got up and walked over to Smiling Eyes and began talking in their language as Prescott and Priscilla remained in their chairs.

Suddenly Smiling Eyes spoke to both Prescott and Priscilla at the same time.

"You can relax now. Our course is set and we will be on our way to Earth at Warp 7 in thirty minutes. The reactor was tweaked during the upgrade and we are able to increment the warp jumps as you call them much faster than this ship's original reactor design."

"What is your occupational specialty Smiling Eyes if I may ask?" Priscilla inquired.

"I was trained as a translator to monitor Earth's languages from transmissions we receive from our ships on Earth and from your internet and from radio and television signals."

"That's why you can speak English a lot better than the other Greys," Prescott commented.

"That's correct."

"What other Earth languages can you speak, or understand?"

"I can understand Russian and speak it fairly well. Mandarin Chinese is proving to be a challenge. My Hebrew is progressing. What makes it especially difficult is that all of these languages use different rules. We have a functional understanding of dozens of Earth's languages."

"Wow," Prescott uttered. "Here you are a Grey and here I am a human you know three Earth languages more than I do."

Smiling Eyes tilted her head upward letting out her high-pitched sound of laughter and was joined by Mind Healer.

Prescott and Priscilla looked at each other grinning and they tilted their heads up laughing too causing Smiling Eyes and Mind Healer to laugh even more.

"Why don't you guys have something to eat?" Mind Healer suggested to Prescott and Priscilla.

"You said 'you guys'," Priscilla observed.

"Is that an incorrect form of the plural second-person pronoun?" Mind Healer wanted to know.

"No," Priscilla said. "Up until now I've only heard you use 'you all' or 'you' for the second plural pronoun."

"I understand 'y'all' is another way to say 'you all' or 'you guys' or 'you' for the second-person plural pronoun," Mind Healer stated.

"It is," Priscilla replied.

Smiling Eyes, who'd been standing nearby, interjected a thought sharing her linguistic expertise.

"English does have a second-person plural using 'you', same as the first-person singular 'you'. English doesn't have a distinct second-person plural pronoun like some other Earth languages."

Prescott had been stumbling around searching for the remaining boxes of his Tongue Scorcher Cracker Snackers.

"Enough with the language lessons," Prescott said in frustration to everyone present, then saying to himself, "Did I eat the rest of my Tongue Scorcher Cracker Snackers?"

Priscilla smiled at Smiling Eyes and gave her a nod, who then temporarily stepped away around the corner.

"Priscilla!" Prescott snarled. "Do you remember if I finished the rest of my Tongue Scorcher Cracker Snackers? I found a box of the regular kind both crispy and easy melt, but no Tongue Scorchers. Oh man, what a bummer."

"Ta da!" Priscilla announced as Smiling Eyes walked in carrying a large box barely allowing her to see over the top of it.

"What's this?" Prescott asked suspiciously.

"Smiling Eyes and I arranged to have 20 bags of 16-ounce Tongue Scorcher Crispy Cracker Snackers made for you at their manufacturing plant, you know the one we took the hovercraft to that day to visit."

Prescott's mouth was hanging open in shock as Priscilla continued her description of her conspiracy with Smiling Eyes.

"I gave Smiling Eyes your last bag of Tongue Scorcher Crispy Cracker Snackers and their chemists and scientists were able to reproduce it perfectly. I swear they taste the same."

Smiling Eyes put down the already opened box as Priscilla opened the top and grabbed a bag and ripped it open.

"Try some," Priscilla said thrusting the unmarked plastic like bag into Prescott's face.

Prescott quickly grabbed a handful and stuffed them in his mouth and began chewing.

"Oh yeah! They're great! Thank you, Smiling Eyes and Priscilla! They even leave the trademark red stain on your fingers."

Smiling Eyes and Mind Healer tilted their heads upward letting out their high-pitched sounds of laughter.

Prescott extended his open bag of Tongue Scorcher Crispy Cracker Snackers to Smiling Eyes and Mind Healer.

"Want some?" Prescott asked.

"I'll pass," Mind Healer said.

Smiling Eyes tentatively put two of her long fingers in the bag and pulled out a couple of cracker snackers and put them in her mouth.

Smiling Eyes bit down and began chewing.

Prescott waited in suspense to get her reaction.

"How do you like my favorite junk food?" Prescott asked.

"Junk food?" Smiling Eyes said quizzically unfamiliar with that term.

"I'll explain later," Priscilla said.

"I like them," Smiling Eyes said as she crunched. "But they get caught between my teeth and they leave red residue on my fingers."

This time Prescott and Priscilla tilted their heads at a 45-degree angle and howled.

"Thank you again, both of you," Prescott said to Priscilla and Smiling Eyes. "This is a very pleasant surprise. I can't believe how good they are. Just like the real thing."

Prescott paused, and then said to Smiling Eyes, "You must give me the recipe."

Smiling Eyes tilted her head upward letting out her high-pitched sound of laughter.

In consideration of the larger size of Prescott and Priscilla the bunks beds, desks, chairs and the dining room table and chairs that had been installed while the saucer was at Area 51 were kept on board during the Grey's upgrade.

"You'd better ration those cracker snackers," Priscilla cautioned Prescott sat at the dining table. "Why couldn't you have asked them to make more than 20 bags?" Prescott asked.

"That was all they could fit into their production run that day. They were slipped in between furniture production runs I was amazed they were able to do it all since that plant made furniture and appliances and didn't process food.

I told Smiling Eyes about the mishap when you tried to heat up and replicate the cracker snackers in the replicator. I have a feeling she already knew about that. They went out of our way for us. They have a specialized food processing plant somewhere else. Be grateful. They had to try several runs before they got it right. I was the taster."

"I apologize. It's a wonderful thing you did. You sure fooled me. I can't figure out when you did it."

"Remember when Smiling Eyes took you to look at the parked hovercraft outside the plant? That's when."

"Got it," he said. "I was wondering why she kept telling me about the engine specs over and over."

Prescott and Priscilla looked at each other knowing it was getting close to bedtime.

"Where are Smiling Eyes and Mind Healer going to sleep?" Priscilla asked.

"I don't know. Maybe the girls will sleep with the girls and the guys will sleep with the guys."

Just at that moment Mind Healer walked up. Prescott remembered a question he wanted to ask.

"We know where sick bay is Mind Healer. Do you have a first aid station? A place like a storage bin with medical supplies?"

"Yes, it's in front of the partition next to what you call sick bay. That was a circuit failure as you would call it that has been fixed."

Mind Healer had a bag with him.

"Smiling Eyes filled me in and I arranged to have prophylactics made for both of you based on your individual physiological constructs."

"In other words, you arranged to have custom birth control made for Priscilla and me."

"I thought I said that," Mind Healer replied.

"Mind Healer," Prescott began, "Where are you sleeping?"

"As you know we don't require sleep in the duration you do. I plan to rest in one of the bunks in one of the bedrooms."

Prescott looked at Priscilla sensing that cultural sensitivity might be in order at this juncture.

"Sit down, please," he told Mind Healer, who complied.

"I'm thinking that you and I would bunk together," Prescott suggested in a friendly manner.

"I will be bunking with my wife," Mind Healer replied calmly.

"You and Smiling Eyes are married?" Priscilla said, almost shouting at Mind Healer.

"Yes. Why?"

"Well, uh," Priscilla sputtered, "I just thought maybe she would have told me."

Prescott was desperately trying not to burst into a fit of laughter. Prescott's right hand was pushing hard against his mouth.

"Gee Priscilla, I guess that means you and I have to bunk together for the next 21 days," Prescott said barely able to get it out before he exploded into raucous laughter.

"Why is Prescott laughing?" Mind Healer wanted to know.

"Because he's a jerk," Priscilla replied, punching his shoulder until she began laughing too.

"I'm glad everyone is happy," Mind Healer said. "We'll be staying in the bedroom closest to the bridge," Mind Healer said as he stood up.

Just before Mind Healer walked away, he got why Prescott was laughing and almost lifted his head up to chuckle, but decided it wasn't that funny and left.

Prescott opened the bag and spilled the contents on the table.

"What do you say? Bunkmates?" Prescott asked Priscilla.

"Bunkmates," she said.

"Good morning baby," Prescott said to Priscilla as he sat a cup of coffee down on the desk in their bedroom. "I've got a cup of coffee for you."

Priscilla stretched.

"Thank you."

Prescott dragged the desk chair over next to Priscilla, who was sleeping on the lower bunk, and put the cup of coffee on it.

Priscilla reached out, grabbed the cup, and took a sip.

"Ah," Priscilla said. "That's good."

"I know what I need to find out today," Prescott said. "I need to find out from Smiling Eyes and Mind Healer how that shower curtain of theirs works. The washer dryer dishwasher and the food replicator oven too."

"We need to find that out," Priscilla concurred. "Don't forget about the trash disposal system and how is that recycled. If we could introduce all that technology on Earth, we could become millionaires fast."

"Yeah, we could," Prescott said, seeing dollar signs dancing in his head.

"They might not want us to have it. It could be classified because it is applicable to other technologies."

"No harm in asking," Prescott quipped.

"Nope, no harm," Priscilla said, taking another sip of her coffee. "It might have a patent. We'd have to pay royalties to somebody on Serpo."

Prescott looked at Priscilla amused at her comment.

"Are we going to continue our journal? Why didn't we keep one when we flew to Serpo?"

"Inertia," Priscilla answered. "I think we were suffering from Post-Traumatic Stress Disorder, PTSD. Yes, we should continue our journal. We can take turns. We got the important stuff already of our two or three or four days on Serpo, or however long it was."

Prescott took Priscilla's cup from her. She hopped out of bed.

"Last night was great," Priscilla said to Prescott as they embraced.

"Same for me times two," he agreed.

They got dressed and walked to the kitchen and had breakfast. Afterwards they joined Smiling Eyes and Mind Healer on the bridge.

"Good morning," Prescott and Priscilla said.

"Good morning," Smiling Eyes and Mind Healer replied.

Priscilla noticed that Smiling Eyes had brought the CD player she had lent Smiling Eyes on the bridge and it was lying on one of the large chairs Prescott and Priscilla sat in when on the bridge.

Smiling Eyes noticed Priscilla was looking at the CD player.

"I've enjoyed listening to the music discs you gave me," Smiling Eyes said appreciatively to Priscilla.

"I heard you playing Bach last night."

"I enjoy Bach. I enjoy listening to the Gregorian Chants. I also found a song by Klaatu on one of the Klaatu discs I like because it reminds my of one of my favorite chants on Serpo."

"What song is that?" Priscilla asked, curious.

"Mrs. Toad's Cookies," Smiling Eyes replied.

Smiling Eyes walked over to the chair, picked up the CD player, forwarded the CD to the song 'Mrs. Toad's Cookies' and pressed the play button.

The song 'Mrs. Toad's Cookies' started.

Smiling Eyes waved her elongated hand and fingers motioning for Mind Healer to join her in a dance.

Smiling Eyes and Mind Healer began dancing around rotating in a choreographed ritual moving to the beat of the song, 'Mrs. Toad's Cookies'.

Priscilla and Prescott joined them dancing by mimicking the movements of Smiling Eyes and Mind Healer.

Mrs. Toad baked some cookies
And Mr. Toad had a ball
But when he finished eating the green sugar cookies
Well his tummy couldn't hold them all
Oh no
No his tummy couldn't hold them all
And he said
Ooh good is good and bad is bad
As any baker knows
But too too much good can be as sadly sad
As too much bad you know
Mrs. Crow fancied flowers
She picked them in fields windblown
But when she'd filled her vases with beautiful blossoms
Well there wasn't any left to grow
Oh no
No there wasn't any left to grow
And she said
Ooh good is good and bad is bad
As any gardener knows
But too too much good can be as sadly sad
As too much bad you know
Do you wonder will tomorrow be a better place
Well that only time can show
But if we put our heads into a better space
Then maybe we could make it so
Oh
Mrs. Toad baked some cookies

And Mr. Toad had a ball
But when he finished eating the green sugar cookies
Well his tummy couldn't hold them all
Oh no
No his tummy couldn't hold them all
And we say
Ooh good is good and bad is bad
As anybody knows
But too too much good can be as sadly sad
As too much bad you know

Prescott and Priscilla and Smiling Eyes and Mind Healer gave themselves high fives and high fours.

Prescott and Priscilla were laughing as Smiling Eyes and Mind Healer had their heads angled upward emitting their special brand of high-pitched laughing.

"One more time!" Prescott said as Priscilla turned the CD back to 'Mrs. Toad's Cookies'.

They all danced and frolicked again to 'Mrs. Toad's Cookies'.

It had been ten days since they left Serpo leaving eleven more days until they reached Earth.

Smiling Eyes was in front of the wall oven having promised to make Prescott and Priscilla a special dish that was beloved on Serpo. Mind Healer was hovering over the oven with Smiling Eyes talking to her in their humming language.

"When are you going to ask them about how that shower curtain of theirs works?" Priscilla asked Prescott. "You also wanted to know how the washer dryer dishwasher and the trash disposal system work."

"After dinner," Prescott said. "I plan to put all my knowledge of human behavior to work. I didn't get a master's degree in psychology for nothing."

"But they're not human," Priscilla stated.

"I have a feeling that they are subject to the same basic motivations and emotions as humans. We'll see."

"Here we are," Smiling Eyes said as she sat a large pot on the table.

Mind Healer and Smiling Eyes stepped on small step ladders positioned in front of their chairs to easily sit down. Their legs dangled over the chairs several inches from the floor.

"What do we have here?" Prescott asked Smiling Eyes as she spooned portions of the dish from the large pot into individual plates and began passing them around.

"You had it at the banquet. I call it jambalaya because you wouldn't be able to pronounce it in our language. It is similar."

"Right, jambalaya," Prescott, said as Priscilla passed him his plate. Prescott, as well as Priscilla, had purposefully come to dinner with an appetite and were very hungry to make it easier to eat the dish in case it turned out to be less than palatable.

They took their first bites and looking at each other began chewing enthusiastically. It was scrumptious if a bit heavy on the spices.

"Now I remember," Prescott said spooning up a large second bite. "It's delicious."

Smiling Eyes looked on with satisfaction that Priscilla and Prescott were enjoying their food. Mind Healer was already half-way finished eating his.

"It has a combination of what is rice for us and our equivalent to onions and tomatoes and celery," Smiling Eyes said. "It also has our chicken equivalent that we added. We are mostly vegetarians, although we do have meat eaters too. I enjoy meat from time to time like now.

Mind Healer almost programmed the oven to make actual Earth or what you might call Cajun or Creole Louisiana jambalaya, but we decided to go with our version."

Prescott and Mind Healer had finished their jambalaya and were holding their plates out to Smiling Eyes for seconds.

"Would everyone like some cranberry juice?" Priscilla asked.

They all nodded as she went to the kitchen to grab four glasses and pour the cranberry juice.

Now that everyone was settled in enjoying their food Prescott thought this would be a good time to ask about the shower curtain as Priscilla gave everyone a glass of cranberry juice.

Looking at Smiling Eyes and Mind Healer, Prescott asked began asking questions in rapid fire fashion.

"How is it you can't see through your shower curtains, yet solid objects like humanoid bodies can walk through them? How does your replicator manage to replicate the molecular pattern of food, store the pattern in memory somehow and use it later to make an exact, or almost an exact, duplicate at will? What is the technology and software behind those washer dryer dishwasher combos? Do you use recycled trash as the baseline matter for the food replicator? How do you do it?"

"It's all what you call classified technology," Mind Healer said. "If I knew I couldn't tell you. But I don't know. It's a closely guarded secret like the formulas for Coca-Cola and KFC original recipe for chicken on your planet."

Prescott and Priscilla laughed at Mind Healer's analogy.

"I told you," Priscilla said to Prescott.

Prescott leaned back in his chair having finished his second helping of Grey or Eben jambalaya.

"I suppose that's that," Prescott uttered in disappointment.

"Smiling Eyes," Priscilla ventured, changing the subject. "At the sendoff speech before we left for Earth the official said your last name and Mind Healer's last name, which are different. In your culture, do you keep your original surnames after marriage?"

"Yes," Smiling Eyes said. "To be more precise, the child decides when they reach the age of accountability which last name to take the mother's or the father's based on a number of factors. Sometimes the surnames for married couples are combined for what you would call legal reasons."

Prescott poised a question.

"Priscilla told me your way of life reflects what Earth's famous economic philosopher said would be the end state of an ideal communist society. His name was Karl Marx."

"I'm familiar with Marx," Mind Healer said. "During the Cold War between America and the Soviet Union we received transmissions about the economic competition between the different production systems communism and capitalism and managed to find out a lot about Marx. Our society has attributes from both Karl Marx and Adam Smith. As I'm sure you saw on Serpo we have an egalitarian society."

"You don't use money, correct?" Priscilla asked both Smiling Eyes and Mind Healer.

"Correct," Smiling Eyes confirmed.

"If you don't have a store of value, how do you know how much something is valued at? How do you know what to make for the coming year? Do you barter goods and services?"

"We've brought along extensive briefing books we plan to provide to all of Earth's leaders when we reach Earth," Smiling Eyes said mysteriously. "These briefing books will answer most questions. I am not able to share the contents of them with you."

"I understand."

"Do you and Mind Healer have children?" Priscilla asked Smiling Eyes.

"Yes, a daughter," Smiling Eyes answered. "We hope she will be accepted into the training school for doctors so she can be a doctor like her father."

"Medical school you could say," Priscilla said.

"Yes," Mind Healer said.

"How do you all like the cranberry juice?" Prescott asked.

"Tasty," Mind Healer said as he drained his glass.

Smiling Eyes asked Priscilla for a refill.

Smiling Eyes and Mind Healer required only a quarter of the amount of sleep Prescott and Priscilla needed.

Smiling Eyes and Mind Healer were far more familiar with the ship than Prescott and Priscilla.

For these two reasons Prescott and Priscilla spent the last week of their journey doing nothing but relaxing and preparing themselves mentally for returning to Earth.

The days went by quickly as Prescott and Priscilla were excited and terrified at the same time by the prospect of returning to Earth.

Mind Healer judiciously dispensed anti-anxiety medication to Prescott and Priscilla and held several therapy sessions with them.

Now they were two days away from Earth.

NORTH AMERICAN AEROSPACE DEFENSE COMMAND (NORAD) NEAR COLORADO SPRINGS, COLORADO

"Sir, the object is approaching at a high rate of speed and should reach Earth's atmosphere in two days.

We've managed to decipher the following message:

START

Our names are Smiling Eyes Drumdordrumdor and Mind Healer Laolellaolel. We are authorized ambassadors representing the government of the planet you call Serpo that orbits around the star you call Zeta 2 Reticuli.

Our government wishes to establish formal diplomatic relations with all countries of the Earth. We bring with us rich secrets of the universe and technology that can transform Earth in a positive way.

Our only condition for establishing diplomatic relations is that the humans called Prescott Barr and Priscilla Waterford be held harmless in any charges that may have been adjudicated against them because they took a spacecraft from the base called Area 51.

We also request that any officials who worked with Prescott Barr and Priscilla Waterford during their employment at Area 51 also be held harmless for any charges that may have been filed against them for negligence.

The spacecraft Prescott Barr and Priscilla Waterford took belonged to and still belongs to the people of Serpo and we consider it a legal fact that they returned property that always belonged to us and therefore can't be considered stolen when it was returned to their rightful owners the people of Serpo.

Please respond in 24 Earth hours. If this is acceptable, we would like to land at the place on Earth known as Area 51 in Nevada.

You may reply to this message as if it was a common radio or television signal and we will receive the transmission within minutes. STOP"

The general in charge roared, "Connect me with The White House now!"

A BRIEFING ROOM IN A BUNKER DEEP UNDERGROUND IN WASHINGTON, D.C. – AN EIGHT HOUR CONFERENCE CALL WITH DOZENS OF WORLD LEADERS HAS JUST ENDED

The President of the United States was relaying final instructions to key civilian and military leaders of the administration.

"Now that the message has been transmitted to the alien ship the next step is to prepare Area 51 for the landing. Since most people on Earth already know about the approaching alien ship, we must secure the desert around Area 51 near the landing site."

The President paused, then turned to one advisor and said, "Do what you can to keep the markets calm."

Smiling Eyes' message had been relayed in Arabic, Basque, Bengali, Bulgarian, Burmese, Cantonese Chinese, Czech, Danish, Dari, Dutch, Edo, English, Estonian, Filipino, Finnish, French, Gaelic, German, Greek, Hausa, Hebrew, Hindi, Hungarian, Igbo, Indonesian, Irish, Italian, Japanese, Javanese, Khmer, Korean, Lao, Latvian, Lithuanian, Macedonian, Malay, Malaysian, Maltese, Mandarin Chinese, Marathi,

Norwegian, Pashto, Persian, Polish, Portuguese, Punjabi, Romanian, Russian, Serbo-Croatian, Slovak, Slovene, Spanish, Swahili, Swedish, Tagalog, Tajik, Teluga, Thai, Turkish, Ukrainian, Urdu, Vietnamese, Wu Chinese, Yoruba, Yue Chinese.

Smiling Eyes was covering the helm and navigation as Mind Healer was sitting in the captain's chair.

Prescott and Priscilla were behind Mind Healer quietly sitting next to each other in dining room chairs they'd brought to the bridge that had been rigged up with seat belts for the landing.

They were holding hands.

Mind Healer turned around and looked at Prescott and Priscilla seeing their anxious faces.

"Are you taking your meds on time and in the correct dosage?" Mind Healer asked.

"Yes," they both replied.

"Incoming message from Earth!" Smiling Eyes cried out excitedly.

"Put it on ship-wide audio," Mind Healer directed.

A computer-like voice similar in sound to the way Prescott and Priscilla heard Mind Healer and Smiling Eyes spoke to them in English was heard all over the saucer.

"To Ambassadors Smiling Eyes Drumdordrumdor and Mind Healer Laolellaolel in the approaching ship from Serpo from all the nations of the Earth, welcome.

The government of the United States of America agrees to your request to hold harmless Prescott Barr and Priscilla Waterford on their acquisition of your spacecraft.

The government of the United States of America also agrees to hold harmless officials who trained and worked with Prescott Barr and Priscilla Waterford during their employment at Area 51.

We agree to your landing at Area 51 to establish diplomatic relations.

Landing coordinates and details to follow in another message to be transmitted within ten minutes."

Prescott and Priscilla leaped from their chairs jumping up and down in ecstatic happiness as Smiling Eyes and Mind Healer joined them in a group hug.

Prescott and Priscilla turned to each other and blurted out simultaneously, "Will you marry me?"

Then holding each other's hands, they simultaneously said, "Yes!"

They laughed and screamed and hugged as Smiling Eyes and Mind Healer tilted their heads upward and let out an especially long high-pitched laugh.

Smiling Eyes telepathed a private message to Mind Healer, "I always knew those two would get married."

Priscilla picked up her CD player and forwarded the Klaatu album to the song 'Magentalane' and pressed play.

Prescott, Priscilla, Mind Healer and Smiling Eyes began slow dancing and swaying around together to the Klaatu song 'Magentalane'.

My my what a lovely day
Could it be that we've arrived in fair Magentalane
There were times, many times
When I thought we wouldn't make it
I was quite prepared to take it like a man
But here I am
Aye aye bring our best champagne
We'll drink a toast, you and I, to fair Magentalane
Now let me see well shouldn't I make a speech
Or say something in Greek
Perhaps recite a Browning poem, but why
When the only thing that's on my mind is
It feels so good
It feels so good
It feels so good
It feels so good

It feels so good to be back at home
In Magentalane
Where the sea of pink champagne flows
Magentalane
Under rose-colored bainrows
I mean rainbows
Yes, there were times, several times
I was sure we'd been defeated
As our Hopes became depleted through the years
But now we're here
So, if you please it's time, we took our leave
The road to liberty awaits us on the aerodrome incline
Gonna leave that bad old world behind
'Cause it feels so good
It feels so good
It feels so good
It feels so good
It feels so good to be back at home

The saucer had deaccelerated to impulse power as it entered the sun's solar system passing Pluto and then Neptune coming up on Uranus.

"We will be entering Earth's atmosphere in a few minutes," Mind Healer said.

Prescott and Priscilla were shivering with excitement as Smiling Eyes pointed to the viewscreen.

"There's Earth," Smiling Eyes said.

They could see the Earth and the moon beginning to fill the viewscreen.

"Going to minimal thrusters," Smiling Eyes said as her long fingers worked the helm and navigation controls.

"Landing coordinates set using the data in the transmission sent from Earth," Smiling Eyes reported. "We'll be over Area 51 in three minutes."

"Raise shields," Mind Healer ordered, "In case they've changed their minds."

"Acknowledged," Smiling Eyes replied engaging the ship's shields.

"Raising shields is a standard operating procedure," Mind Healer said, looking at Prescott and Priscilla.

Prescott quickly whispered to Priscilla, "Shields weren't part of the flight simulator training."

Mind Healer overheard Prescott and provided an explanation.

"Shields on this ship were damaged during its last visit to Earth and we have minimal documentation on it. That's why you didn't find anything about them listed in your translation documents."

The North American continent came into view.

"Locking in automatic controls to the Area 51 landing site coordinates," Smiling Eyes said.

"Switching to bottom view," Smiling Eyes reported as the saucer hovered just outside Earth's atmosphere ready to descend to Area 51 and the designated landing site.

Prescott and Priscilla were standing just behind Smiling Eyes enraptured and gazing intently at the viewscreen.

"Take your seats and fasten your belts," Mind Healer ordered Prescott and Priscilla, who sat down in the dining room chairs and did as they were instructed.

Prescott and Priscilla could feel the saucer quickly going down as they saw the Rocky Mountains and desert areas of the western United States coming into view.

"Look Prescott there's Tucson and Phoenix and Las Vegas," Priscilla cooed is awe. "Amazing," Prescott whispered his eyes wide.

The saucer hovered after going a bit north of Las Vegas and began a slow descent.

As the saucer approached Area 51 Prescott and Priscilla and Smiling Eyes and Mind Healer could see tens of thousands of people with an equivalent number of vehicles of all kinds strewn across the desert.

"We have a welcoming party," Mind Healer said, leaning his head forward to take in the spectacle.

"Ready on deacceleration thrusters," Smiling Eyes said.

Prescott and Priscilla watched as the saucer veered slightly toward an open area away from the thousands of people in the desert.

Smiling Eyes' long fingers expertly worked the helm and navigation controls.

"Unbelievable," Prescott and Priscilla kept saying as they surveyed the tremendous number of people who had gathered in the desert for their return.

"Extending landing supports," Smiling Eyes reported.

"Landing impact in thirty seconds," Smiling Eyes said beginning a countdown using Earth time for Prescott's and Priscilla's sake.

Prescott and Priscilla watched in utter fascination as the desert ground surged forward.

"Ten, five and touchdown," Smiling Eyes said.

The saucer came to a stop resting on the ground.

"We made it! We're here!" Prescott and Priscilla began shouting unbuckling their seat belts and springing out of their chairs.

Smiling Eyes and Mind Healer unbuckled their seat belts and stood together speaking in their humming language happy to see Prescott and Priscilla so happy.

"Are you ready?" Smiling Eyes said. "Your public awaits," Smiling Eyes added, using what she knew was an idiom appropriate for this auspicious occasion.

"Our public awaits you mean," Prescott corrected her.

Prescott and Priscilla hugged Smiling Eyes and Mind Healer crying and whispering thank you repeatedly into what passed for their ears.

Mind Healer as the Captain took charge.

"Open the door hatch," Mind Healer told Smiling Eyes.

"Our public awaits us," Mind Healer said as he and the other three walked out of the bridge, down the corridor and stood just inside the opened door hatch.

After humming with Smiling Eyes for a few seconds, Mind Healer said to Prescott and Priscilla, "You two go out first."

Prescott and Priscilla stepped out of the hatch door into bright sunshine and began walking down the ramp waving as a deafening roar from thousands and thousands of people filled the desert air as Smiling Eyes and Mind Healer followed behind.

An extremely large military contingent surrounded the landing area as helicopters circled overhead. Two pairs of jets could be seen flying in formation over Area 51.

All four stopped at the bottom of the ramp as the President of the United States accompanied by a dozen world leaders began walking toward them.

Prescott, Priscilla, Smiling Eyes and Mind Healer had all discussed the protocol they would follow immediately after landing. They had decided Smiling Eyes would step forward first to greet the Earth delegation as the officially designated ambassador and representative of the government and people of the planet Serpo.

Smiling Eyes stepped forward.

"Welcome to Earth," the President said to Smiling Eyes as they both shook hands.

"We are honored to be here," Smiling Eyes said, communicating telepathically as she was shaking hands with other world leaders and exchanging pleasantries.

Smiling Eyes turned around and motioned for Prescott and Priscilla and Mind Healer to join her.

As Prescott and Priscilla were shaking hands, they saw several other people walking forward including many familiar faces. Colonel Smith, Bob, Jim, Roger, Susan and many others joined the greeting party.

"Colonel Smith," Prescott and Priscilla said emotionally, "We're so sorry about what we did."

"Let's not talk about it," Colonel Smith replied good naturedly. "Since we knew you were coming back, we've all become heroes. Me and Bob and Jim and Roger and Susan and everybody are credited with preparing you for your diplomatic mission to Serpo. That's the official cover story. You'll be briefed on it later."

Prescott and Priscilla hugged Colonel Smith, then hugged all of their coworkers at Area 51 whom they had betrayed and had left Earth as thieves and traitors, only to return to Earth as heroes and friends.

Tears of happiness were flowing in abundant amounts all around.

An elaborate military and security contingent had been hurriedly thrown together to protect the important dignitaries and world leaders assembled to greet the visitors from Serpo, as well as Prescott and Priscilla.

To the relief of everyone, the huge crowd in the desert surrounding the landing site was as disciplined, as quiet and as respectful as a crowd attending the annual Masters Golf Tournament in Augusta, Georgia.

The enormous crowd was stunned into awed silence aware of being present at a momentous day and event in recorded human history.

Prescott, Priscilla, Smiling Eyes and Mind Healer attended many debriefings, meetings and diplomatic functions under tight security.

They were all flown to New York where Smiling Eyes spoke to a General Assembly of the United Nations. They were all honored by the U.N.

Then they were all flown to Washington D.C. where Smiling Eyes spoke to a Joint Session of Congress. They were all presented with Presidential Medal of Freedoms by the President of the United States.

One week later.

Prescott and Priscilla were leaving another debriefing at Area 51 with Smiling Eyes and Mind Header.

Smiling Eyes and Mind Header were scheduled to return to Serpo in five days.

"Let's go to the canteen and have a late lunch," Priscilla asked Smiling Eyes and Mind Healer. Mind Healer hummed with Smiling Eyes and said, "Why not?"

They all four stood in line like everyone else. The workers at Area 51 had already become used to seeing Smiling Eyes and Mind Healer walking around. They no longer attracted any special attention from the rank and file.

FBI agents were planted within the workforce and were keeping a close eye on things including Prescott and Priscilla and most importantly Smiling Eyes and Mind Healer.

Priscilla ordered split pea soup and BLT sandwiches for Smiling Eyes and Mind Header, along with orange sodas. Prescott and Priscilla ordered the same for themselves.

"If you pay for lunch, I'll cover the tip," Smiling Eyes said to Prescott, then tilting her head up she let out a long laugh. Prescott was momentarily nonplussed, until he remembered he'd said the same thing to Smiling Eyes on Serpo about her buying breakfast and his covering the tip.

"That's funny Smiling Eyes!" Prescott said, slapping Smiling Eyes on the back pushing her forward a little.

"Oh, sorry, are you ok?" Prescott asked her with concern.

"I'll have to check with my attorney," Smiling Eyes replied. "I may want to press charges," Smiling eyes said, then lifted her head up again joined by Mind Healer as they had a belly laugh.

Prescott winked at Priscilla as they quickly walked away with their trays leaving Smiling Eyes and Mind Healer with an expectant cashier who said to Smiling Eyes, "That'll be $20.88."

Prescott and Priscilla sat their trays down at a table as Prescott sprinted back and paid the cashier as Smiling Eyes and Mind Healer joined Prescott and Priscilla.

Mind Healer was digging into his BLT. "This is tasty," Mind Healer said as Smiling Eyes tried the split pea soup.

"How do you like the soup?" Priscilla asked Smiling Eyes. "Interesting. I think I like it," she said taking a second spoonful.

Priscilla looked at Prescott and then at Smiling Eyes.

"Smiling Eyes, as you know Prescott and I are getting married on Saturday. You are scheduled to leave the following Monday. Even though you are married I want you to be my maid of honor."

Smiling Eyes put her spoon down. "I would be honored. I assume the maid of honor is a position of honor at a human wedding. Is the maid of honor supposed to be unmarried?"

"On Earth the tradition is the maid of honor is unmarried, but we'll make an exception in your case. You'll have to be measured for a bridal dress if that's ok."

"That will be ok. I hope I will know how to wear a dress," Smiling Eyes said. "Don't worry about that leave it to me," Priscilla reassured her.

Prescott then looked at Mind Healer, who had finished his BLT and was reaching his four long fingers toward Smiling Eyes' BLT, who pushed his hand away.

"Want another BLT?" Prescott asked Mind Healer.

"Yes, I enjoyed it very much."

"You got it bro," Prescott said. "I'll get you another one in a minute. I have a favor, a question to ask you."

"Yes?" Mind Healer said.

"I'd like you to be my best man at the wedding on Saturday. It's taking place at the Luxor Hotel in Las Vegas. It's where Priscilla and I had our first date."

"I would be honored," Mind Healer said. "Is the best man a similar task like the maid of honor?"

"In a way," Prescott replied. "It's for the groom. Me."

"I understand. Is there anything special I need to do?"

"Wear a tuxedo and tie and hand me the ring when the preacher gives us the high sign."

"High sign?"

"Never mind. We'll discuss the details on Saturday. Let me get you that BLT."

Prescott and Priscilla were in her apartment on Friday going over the final planning and preparations for their wedding.

"Colonel Smith assured me he'll have Smiling Eyes and Mind Healer at the Luxor by noon tomorrow," Prescott said to Priscilla, who was going over her checkoff list.

"Smiling Eyes looks cute in her dress," Priscilla said remembering the uproar when she and Smiling Eyes visited a bridal shop under heavy guard.

Prescott chuckled. "Mind Healer looks pretty sharp in a tuxedo."

The FBI was highly annoyed by the uproar surrounding the wedding that caused them no end of logistical and security protection procedure nightmares. They were asked by the President of the United States to use extreme tolerance in accommodating requests of this nature involving the aliens and Prescott and Priscilla.

Priscilla remembered the dropped placard that listed the names of a couple that had just been married at the Luxor Hotel. They were Norma and Ralph of Spendler Shoes in Henderson, Nevada.

She called Spendler Shoes and invited Norma Kasabian-Dumas and Ralph Dumas to their wedding and Norma and Ralph accepted. Norma also accepted on behalf of Donna Diligent, who had briefly spoken to them in front of the Luxor Hotel and who had been the one who had dropped the placard.

Norma, Ralph and Donna were thrilled to be able to attend the wedding of world-famous and history making celebrities.

In addition to Prescott's and Priscilla's parents and siblings, Colonel Smith, Bob, Jim, Roger, Susan and a dozen other coworkers from Area 51 would also be in attendance at their wedding.

Prescott and Priscilla were married at the Luxor Hotel in Las Vegas on Saturday.

Smiling Eyes was Priscilla's maid of honor and Mind Healer was Prescott's best man.

The preacher was conducting the wedding ceremony.

"Please take the ring you have selected for Prescott Barr. As you place it on his finger, repeat after me: 'With this ring, I thee wed'."

"With this ring, I thee wed," Priscilla said as she placed the ring on Prescott's finger.

"Please take the ring you have selected for Priscilla Waterford. As you place it on her finger, repeat after me: 'With this ring, I thee wed'."

Mind Healer nimbly handed Prescott the ring with his long fingers.

"With this ring, I thee wed," Prescott said as he placed the ring on Priscilla's finger.

"In so much as the two of you have consented together in holy wedlock, and have witnessed the same before God and this company, by the authority vested in me by the State of Nevada, I now pronounce you husband and wife. You may kiss the bride!"

Donna, who'd briefly spoken with Prescott and Priscilla on the night of Norma's and Ralph's wedding, turned to all who were within earshot and said, "I always knew those two would get married."

Prescott and Priscilla delayed their honeymoon until after Smiling Eyes' and Mind Healer's departure back to Serpo.

They all made a quick trip to see the Grand Canyon and Hoover Dam. Smiling Eyes and Mind Healer were impressed. Everyone had a great time including the FBI agents assigned to guard and protect them.

Before Smiling Eyes and Mind Healer left Earth to return to Serpo, Prescott and Priscilla had an emotional farewell with them.

They exchanged contact information and took dozens of photos and selfies.

For the first time Prescott and Priscilla saw Smiling Eyes and Mind Healer cry.

Prescott and Priscilla cried too.

Chapter 17

In the Beginning

Two hours before Smiling Eyes and Mind Healer were scheduled to take off from Area 51 and return to Serpo a top-secret meeting was held.

Invited to this meeting were religious leaders representing the world's religious faiths.

Smiling Eyes and Mind Healer were standing at a podium in front of a projection screen. A large box they had brought with them was on the podium.

Smiling Eyes began speaking.

"We've brought you many ideas for technical and societal advancement that can benefit Earth's many cultures. The most important truth we have brought with us is described on one slide we are about to show you. Supplementary information is contained in this box on the stage."

The room was darkened, the projector was turned on and the slide displayed on the screen.

The audience gasped in astonishment.

www.ingramcontent.com/pod-product-compliance
Lightning Source LLC
LaVergne TN
LVHW091545060526
838200LV00036B/706